# Mimi of the



A Chapter in the Chronicles of the Great Migration

MIMI OF THE NOWHERE

First edition. May 17, 2018.



Publisher: Loridian's Laboratory LLC
Ebook edition ISBN: 978-1732357600
Print Edition ISBN 978-1732357617
Written by Michael Kilman
Cover Art by:
Gabriel Perez
https://www.artofgp.com/
Cover Titles by:
Desiree Byrd
Edited By:
Vanessa Corn
https://vcedits.com/

# Chapter 1
# The Fishing Hole

THE SHARPENED END OF the broomstick plunged down below the waterline with a *plunk*.

"It's hard to believe there's any fish down here," said Shannon.

"Best way to manage the algae," Mimi said with a grunt. She pulled up the broomstick, free of fish, dripping water.

"Really? But I thought they wanted the algae to bloom for the biorecycler."

Mimi's eyes danced over the surface of the water, tracing the shadow of a fish just visible in the dim underground light.

"Algae grows better with the fish."

"Why's that?"

The broomstick handle brushed the surface of the water, roaming back and forth. Then, she thrusted, quick and sharp. When she pulled out her makeshift spear, a fish flopped back and forth, gasping for freedom. Mimi swung the end upward to keep the fish from sliding off.

She shrugged. "Hell if I know. Something about ecology or some nonsense."

Mimi knew. She knew a lot of things she shouldn't know. She had skimmed the knowledge from a sanitation worker, one who managed the algae pools.

"What's ecology?"

Mimi shrugged. She shifted the broom from one hand to the other and brushed her long black hair out of her eyes. "It's not important. We best get out of here, maintenance is coming."

"How do you know that?" asked Shannon. "How do you always know stuff like that?"

"They usually come around this time. Come on, we have dinner. Let's go cook it." She was lying. There was no set schedule down here. The only time someone showed up was when there was a problem.

They walked away from the stream, moving up the long tunnel and toward the main pond. It was hard to call it a pond, because it was larger than Central Park and it branched out in streams to several other parts of the excavated piece of earth on which the great walking city of Manhatsten rested.

"You can really feel the legs moving down here, can't you?"

"Every step. Gotta be careful, takes a while to get your sea legs."

"Sea legs?"

Mimi shrugged. "Nevermind." She liked Shannon, but she asked too many questions. Mimi didn't like questions. When you were homeless in a giant walking city, questions could get you killed. Yet, she always seemed to pick the ones who asked a lot of questions. Where were all her previous partners? She didn't like to think about it.

She glanced up at Shannon's face; she was pale and slender, almost the exact opposite of the last woman she had dated. Her soft brown eyes caught Mimi staring at her. Her narrow face and blonde hair were lovely in the dim light of the underground.

"What?"

"Nothing, you just look beautiful today."

Shannon smiled and her face flushed a little. She reached out and grabbed Mimi's hand. Mimi never failed to notice how much bigger Shannon's hand was. Of course, Shannon was of a normal size, while Mimi was tiny.

"I'm glad you asked me to come down here and see this place. I didn't even know it existed."

Mimi said, "Only a few people outside of the sanitation workers do."

They reached the edge of the pond and Mimi looked over it. It was quiet. Only the sound of the water lapping against the edge of the land was prominent, interspersed with slim moments of the noise of the machinery pumping water in and out of the massive reservoir.

Shannon moved closed to her. She could feel her body pressed up against hers. It was soft and warm. Mimi took a slow breath, enjoying the feeling. She tucked her head into Shannon's chest and took a moment to listen to her heart and linger in her scent.

Shannon said, "It's kind of a turn-on being down here...all hidden and forbidden, I mean."

Mimi smiled and looked up into her face. "Yes, but as I said, someone is coming." She leaned in and kissed Shannon for a moment, then took her hand and led her further along the shoreline, back to the entrance where they had come.

It had been a long time since Mimi had felt close to someone. The last time had been several decades before. Over the centuries, she brought several partners down here. It was one of her favorite places in the whole city. It was almost always safe from the security patrols and the drug dealers in the lowers.

There wasn't a lot of room to explore on the streets of Manhastan, but down here...down here was nowhere. Down here was *her* nowhere.

The garbled thoughts of the maintenance workers were clarifying. It meant they were getting closer. The clearer she could hear thoughts, the closer someone was. At a few dozen yards' distance, she could make out everything that was on the surface of a person's mind, assuming there was only a few of them.

It was the other reason she liked being down here; she had quiet inside and out.

Suddenly, the minds clarified. They were moving quickly. She couldn't understand why. Her heart raced; they would be on top of them at any moment.

"Shit, they're coming now." Mimi grabbed Shannon by the shoulder and pulled her behind a giant metal tube, one of many scattered around the perimeter of the pond. She could feel and hear a low hum coming from the tube.

"How do you know—"

Mimi put her hand over Shannon's mouth. "Shh. If they hear us, we're in deep shit."

Mimi felt Shannon's body relax for a moment. Then, as the elevator door across the pond spilled light out onto the choppy water and two sanitation workers stepped out, she felt Shannon's body tense again. They were still more than a kilometer away, but if they had been out in the open, it would have been obvious.

The elevator. Of course. That was the reason for the sudden movement. Mimi should have known better. But why was she reading them as if they were much closer? There was no reason she should be able to hear them so clearly from this distance.

Mimi glanced her companion and realized that she had let herself relax a little too much. It was stupid. She should have been paying more attention, even if she was getting an unusually strong read.

Mimi pulled Shannon a little closer. Shannon reached back and gave her bicep a squeeze. It occurred to Mimi that she found a deep sense of joy in feeling Shannon close. It was too late. She was falling hard. That was dangerous.

Mimi whispered in Shannon's ear, "Stay still. We have to wait 'til they pass. We can't make a sound. You know what happened to Tanya, right?"

Without turning, Shannon tensed. She nodded her head.

"Let's move a little further back against this wall. I doubt they'll come this way. They're here to inspect one of the lines on the other side."

Shannon squirmed a little and turned her head. Her hoarse whisper was barely audible. "How do you know all this shit, Mimi?"

Mimi shrugged. She wasn't about to tell Shannon how she knew it, or how she knew anything else. She was falling in love with Shannon, realized that she might even spend the rest of Shannon's life with her, short as that may end up being, but there was no one she could ever trust with her secret, not again. It would never be like it was with Daniel, would it? His was a miserable lesson.

Yet, she was making it obvious that she had secrets. She frowned to herself. All day she had been hinting about knowing information she shouldn't. It occurred to her that maybe, on some level, she wanted someone to know. Maybe she was tired of being alone, maybe she missed waking up next to someone, trusting someone with everything. Lying was tiresome.

The two workers' laughs echoed off the massive chamber. They made no effort to be quiet, and just as they got within a few hundred meters, they stopped. Their thoughts, loud and clear, disappeared. The sudden silence unnerved Mimi.

She reached out. More silence. She pushed a little harder, thinking of them. A bright red light and a powerful ringing in her ears hit her like a physical blow. She shuddered. Her body spasmed.

Shannon turned towards her. "Mimi?"

Mimi released her grip and stepped back, shaking her head and putting her finger to her lips. Shannon understood and turned back towards the workers.

When they moved again, they did so in her direction. Mimi frowned. Why had they changed direction?

Minutes passed. No sign of their minds. No intentions. Just silence and hints of footsteps and murmurs.

Mimi felt her heart beat harder. Sweat gathered on her forehead. She was having trouble breathing. She tried to will their thoughts back again, and that same red light and deafening ringing returned. She needed to know what these two were doing. Uncertainty was death in this world. She had watched through the centuries as so many of her friends and loved ones had been taken by the security forces and sentenced to a fate worse than death.

Only a hundred meters away now, the voices focused from the frame of echoes and clarified in the space. “I don’t know, Frank, I swore I saw something over this direction.”

“Zelda, you kidding me with this shit? Ain’t no one even knows about this place.”

“I didn’t say it was a person, maybe it's a busted pipe or something.”

“It’s almost quitting time.”

The woman stopped and faced the man. The woman was wire-thin, and the man had a large, round belly that almost intruded in the conversation.

“Frank, you know damn well if there is a major issue, we're gonna be down here for weeks cleaning up the mess.”

“So, let’s report we heard some strange noises in the pipes and send someone else down to investigate,” said the man.

Mimi ground her teeth. No minds, only voices. That vacant silence felt as if someone had scooped something essential out of her. So far as she could remember, this had never happened before, not since the voices began. It could mean the end for her and Shannon. Was her future the Runnercore? The remainder of their lives as prisoners out in the barren wasteland that the city traversed, running errands for a society that viewed them as disposable? Or perhaps they would die a brutal death at the hands of another city’s Runners? But then, that was if they were lucky; they could spend centuries in semi-stasis, waiting in storage to be activated.

“It doesn’t hurt to just check it out, Frank. Besides, wouldn’t kill you to work off that gut some.”

There was a pause between the two. The man rubbed his stomach. “What, this old thing? Come on, Zelda, you know I’ve been carefully cultivating this thing for the last twenty years. Why you gotta go and try and go and get me some exercise?” The man laughed at his own joke. It was a deep, booming laugh that bounced off the high walls of the cavern.

It did nothing for Mimi’s nerves.

Shannon started to squirm again, and Mimi gripped her a bit more firmly. She tried to make it a loving, comforting grip, but when she looked down at Shannon’s right wrist, she saw that she was white-knuckled. Shannon’s hand was reddening. She relaxed her grip.

Shannon leaned back and whispered, "What's wrong, I can feel you shaking."

Mimi *was* shaking. Her whole body was betraying her with ripples of gooseflesh. Still, there was mental silence. It was a kind of fog that had climbed its way into her ears.

"Shhhh."

The woman turned in their direction. "Did you hear that?" Her words were crystal-clear now. She was walking directly toward them.

Mimi cursed under her breath. Leaning forward as quietly as she could, she whispered into Shannon's ear, "Get ready to run when I say so."

Shannon tensed under her. She, too, shook.

Why had everything gone silent? It made no sense, unless maybe she was just getting old? Maybe her bizarre skill set withered away with age like anything else? But that made little sense. The regeneration alcove she semi-frequently snuck into rejuvenated all of her cells. Her mental capabilities should have been renewed in the process as well.

The woman was only a few dozen meters away now.

"Zelda, you're killing me. Let's just finish the job we came down for." He was pleading with her. Mimi noted a sense of desperation in his voice. Something about that gave her a renewed sense of hope.

Zelda stopped and turned away. Mimi used that moment to pull Shannon all the way back behind the pipe so that she couldn't see the woman, and the woman couldn't see her.

"I'm telling you, Frank, there's something over there. I'd swear it."

"Bet your next paycheck?"

There was silence for a moment.

"Well... Nah."

"If you ain't gonna put your money where your mouth is, then let's get back to work. The wife's waiting, you know. And she doesn't like it when I'm late all the time, especially when she knows I came down here with you."

There it was. That was why he was pleading.

"Is she still on you about that shit, Frank?"

"Come on, you know some people, once they get an idea, it rubs at them 'til they're raw. She ain't never gonna let it go."

"Jesus Frank, it was one kiss, twenty years ago, and I was drunk."

"Don't matter."

There was silence again for a moment. It was a horrible silence. Mimi hated it. She had never thought she could hate silence so much.

"Alright, fine. You win. Let's get back to it."

Mimi felt all the pressure inside of her release at once. The woman's footsteps sounded as if they were walking away, but it was hard to tell.

Then, all at once, their thoughts flooded her mind again. She didn't know what had turned them back on, but she was grateful. The pair was moving away; they would address a reported blockage on the other side of the pond and suggest that maybe something else was wrong in the area Mimi was hiding. Mimi had never felt so relieved in her life.

She stuck out her head from her cover and watched and waited a few minutes more. She probed the area for any other minds, and when she sensed none, she said, "Come on, all clear."

There were only two ways out of the pond: the elevator and the stairs. No sanitation worker in their right mind would use the stairs; it was 102 levels from the lowest sub-basement to the algae pools. Shannon had moaned the entire way down the stairs about how difficult it would be to come back up. She had complained that her legs were already jelly from going down 102 flights, and Mimi expected her to bitch the whole way up. But as they approached the metal-grated stairs—still keeping their eyes on the ever-more-distant workers—Shannon was silent. They began their ascent.

Mimi turned and looked at her face; it was ghost-pale. Mimi didn't have to skim her mind to know what was wrong. She shouldn't have mentioned Tanya. She wanted her to take the threat seriously, but she didn't want to scare the living shit out of her, either. She imagined that mentioning Tanya probably deepened Shannon's terror as that woman had approached.

Mimi grabbed Shannon's hand and faced her. She tilted her head up and kissed her deeply. Mimi pulled away and stared right into Shannon's eyes.

"I'm sorry. I didn't mean to mention it."

Shannon looked down at the floor. "It's okay... I just... I still can't believe she's gone."

"She's not gone. She's in the Runnercore."

"She's dead."

"No, she's not."

Shannon twirled her hair and chewed on her lip.

"You know what they say about women in the Runnercore."

"Weak women, Shannon. Tanya was bigger and stronger than most women."

"Enough to move in those metal suits? Can you say for certain she's alive?" Shannon was pleading.

Mimi said nothing. She had tried to find out. She had even snuck down to the docks several nights in a row to skim someone. The inspectors weren't helpful, there were just too many Runners to think about, and inspectors didn't know anyone's names. Once you became a Runner, you were just a number, a designation. Unless she could find out what Tanya's designation had become, there was no use. She had tried to probe the Recycled Runners, but they were nothing but empty hard drives. Too empty, like trying to read a brick.

"They augment their muscles, you know."

"What do you mean?"

"I mean they inject them with some kind of hormone or chemical or something. It makes them stronger."

Shannon's eyes squinted, "How do you know that?"

"The same way I know everything else. I listen. If you did as I told you when we are out scavenging, you would know as much as me."

It was a lie. Shannon couldn't skim minds. Mimi wasn't entirely sure if anyone else in the city could, either. As far as she knew, she was all alone. It almost made her laugh when she thought about it. What a great gift to be wasted on a homeless woman. Yet, something had happened this afternoon. Something that made her question if she was alone. Why the red light and the tone? Could someone out there be blocking her?

"Listen, you're just going to have to trust me. Tanya's okay. One of these days, we'll bust her out."

Shannon smiled, the corners of her mouth creeping to their highest altitude. She choked back a laugh. Mimi loved it when she did that.

"Oh right, two bag ladies are going to bust down into the Runner Docks to liberate another bag lady. Sounds like something from the vidscreens." Her smile melted. "Sometimes having hope is foolish, isn't it."

Mimi squeezed her hand, "Crazier things have happened."

"Really? When?"

"Um, we are in what was once bedrock at the base of a giant walking city, aren't we? I think that qualifies as a crazy miracle. Whoever thought up this idea to deal with climate change had to sound like a total nutjob, but they did it, didn't they? They pulled it off, and not just once."

"I guess so." Shannon's voice sounded soft and resigned. "Do you know how many cities are still out there?"

"I don't know. Couldn't be more than a dozen left."

"You think Manhatsten will be around for a while?"

"Hell if I know." She nodded her head towards the stairs. "Come on. I'll race you to the top."

"You're joking, right? I mean, you're really joking?"

"Nope." And Mimi ran up the stairs, taking two at a time.

# Chapter 2
# Home Sweet Home

MIMI WORKED HER WAY through the large, cold pipe on her hands and knees, careful to keep the fish from touching the ground. The weight of it dangling was not great, but she struggled to steady its swaying motion as she shuffled along.

She slid out of the exit into the open area that led to her lair. A giant, metallic cylinder occupied most of the space. It was several stories tall and made a constant humming noise. Its outer shell was marked with rust and age.

Behind her, Shannon slid out of the pipe. Her sneakers slapped against the ground. The impact was almost too much. The sneakers barely hung together, bound by adhesive strips. Her clothes, like Mimi's, were sewn together from discarded bits of cloth they had scavenged from the clothing recycling center.

So much of the city was recycled; it had to be. But the city, approaching the mid-twelfth century of its age, was showing signs of its tireless movement. Only rarely did the city cease walking across the barren landscape, and then it shuddered under the vibration of a massive drill, extracting the scraps of resources that were left in the earth's crust.

"Wow, this is where you live?" asked Shannon. "Yuck." She plugged her nose. "What's that smell?"

"Sewage and garbage. Though there might be other things mixed in there, I'm not sure."

Shannon almost gagged. "Here I thought, we've been together six months and I haven't even been to her place yet. I thought maybe you were hiding something. You were: your place smells like shit."

Mimi laughed. "Shit's only part of it."

"Why does it smell so terrible?"

"Because," Mimi waved her stick toward the giant cylinder. "That's a biorecycler. Well, the bottom half of it, anyway. The other half is up in one of the Sanitation departments."

"But aren't those things supposed to be sealed? Why does it smell so bad?"

"It leaks sometimes."

"What, like, on you?"

"Nah, I'm over on the other side over there." She pointed down a narrow corridor. "I think things would have to be bad in the city before the whole thing emptied. Maybe a war with one of the other cities or something. Besides, it's one of the safest places in the whole city for someone like us."

They walked toward the corridor. Small, iridescent puddles twinkled in the light. Mimi didn't know what all the chemicals were, but she steered Shannon around each one.

"Doesn't smell like it. Why's it so safe?"

"No one comes down here unless there's a major problem. So far, there's been one in the last few hundred years."

Mimi realized her mistake at once and hoped Shannon wouldn't notice. She almost swore out loud. Instead, she held her breath.

Shannon stopped and grabbed Mimi's right arm, the one without the dangling fish. "Wait a second. How. Old. Are. You?"

"Seventy or so." Her words came out rapid fire. She knew she could pass for seventy, though she didn't look a day over the age of twenty-five; it was the product of the regeneration alcoves. Even the homeless had occasional access to them. It was cheaper than dealing with disease and medical care, so the Uppers—the ones who lived in the top floors of the city—had decided to make some alcoves accessible to everyone, but only often enough that someone who was homeless or living in the lower parts of the city could live a maximum lifespan of two-hundred years or so.

"Then how do you know when this thing last broke down?"

"Uh... I looked it up. Come on, it doesn't smell so bad back where I'm at." Mimi knew that wasn't going to cut it, but she couldn't come up with anything else to say.

Shannon followed, but Mimi could tell she was frustrated. She would have to tell her some truth soon at least. Lying all the time was hard. There was so much to keep track of. But how was she going to explain her age? How would she explain that she had found a way to access a regeneration alcove and extend her life like the wealthy Uppers in the city? She knew exactly where that would lead. Daniel had wanted access to the alcoves, and it had cost him everything.

They stepped over the crisscross networks of pipes in one section, ducked under them in another, and moved their way through several cramped areas until, finally, they reached her nest.

It wasn't anything special, but it was a spot to call home. Multicolored sheets patched together tightly to create a sturdy outer covering over a frame of pipes, tucked away in a corner. It was well-hidden. You had to be looking for it to know it was there. Mimi pulled back a flap and ushered Shannon inside. A small, ancient mattress lay on the floor next to a small makeshift camping stove. The mattress also had patches, like a bandaged soldier after a battle. It was lumpy and uneven, but much better than anything they would find at street level. A few tattered maps of the city hung in the corners, displaying the underground networks of tunnels and pipes.

"Where'd you get the furniture and pictures? Some place down here?"

"The furniture, well, you just have to know where to look. Mattresses don't exactly grow in Central Park. The maps I stole from Sanitation. Not like they will miss them."

"What do you need the maps for?"

Mimi shrugged, "Nothing really, anymore. I know most of those tunnels by heart now, but it took a while to get the hang of them."

"So why do you still have them up?"

"Habit, I guess. Better than nothing, right? Makes it feel cozy."

Shannon walked around the room inspecting everything. "Hmmm. I suppose so." She lifted the bottom of one of the maps and looked under, exposing the splotched green and brown cloth below. "Yeah, better with the maps. You need some flowers here or something."

"Flowers? You're joking, right?"

"You could swipe some from Central Park or one of the other green spaces in the city."

Mimi shook her head, "Do you want to attract attention? You know how much those flowers go for in the uppers?"

Shannon shook her head.

"Let's put it this way, you'd probably end up in front of the Supreme Justices."

"For flowers?"

"For flowers."

"So, you've never picked any?"

"No, have you?"

"No, but they smell so nice. I just thought that..." Shannon trailed off.

Mimi shrugged. "Think whatever you want, the point is, getting the attention of the Security Officers for flowers seems like a waste."

"But in the vidscreens... when a girl brings another flowers, it's so romantic."

"That's the vidscreens. Those programs are all about Mids and Uppers, anyway. No one wants to hear love stories about a couple of homeless women."

Shannon frowned.

Mimi reached over and pressed a few buttons to prime the makeshift stove. She pulled the fish off her broom handle and flopped it down on the grill. She turned around and pulled out a wide and flat piece of metal with a wooden handle. It was bound together by some cheap twine.

"What's that?" Shannon stared at the object.

"You ever gut a fish before?"

"Gut?"

"Yeah, gut. You can't just plop it on a grill and cook, you know. You gotta take out the guts, cut off the head."

"Ew, what?" Shannon's nose wrinkled. Her face paled.

"I'll show you." Mimi grabbed the fish and stepped outside her dwelling. She found a flat surface and Shannon, following reluctantly, watched as she raised the blade and brought it down just south of the fish's head. It made a soft squishing sound, and a little of the creature's juices sprayed onto both women.

Shannon's eyes widened, and she pushed past Mimi. She ran around a corner and vomited.

Afterward, Shannon refused to eat the fish. Mouth full, Mimi said, "You can't be so squeamish about things down here. You have to eat what you can get or you'll go hungry."

Shannon said nothing. She kept looking at the maps, kept looking at the ancient sheets that were tied to the pipes. Her hand caressed them. Then, keeping her eyes off of the fish, she stared right at Mimi.

"Alright, how old are you, really? And don't give me that seventy crap. Besides, you look way too young for seventy anyway, even with our alcove allotment. It's clear you're a lot older than that."

Mimi shrugged. "Women of Asian descent just age slowly." She paused for a moment. "Tomorrow we'll take another trip down below. There's a food dispenser down there I can hack sometimes, if you don't like the fish."

"Don't change the subject. You have access to an alcove, don't you?"

Mimi swallowed her last bite of the fish. "Sure you're not going to eat?"

Shannon shook her head and gestured for Mimi to eat the rest.

"Answer me, please, or I'm leaving."

"Come on now, Shannon, don't say that. I love you."

Shannon was almost sidetracked by this. Her face lit up. "You do?" Then her face darkened a little. "You love me, do you? But not enough to tell me the truth?" Shannon shifted her body in the chair, the little table wobbling off balance. "You're always lying to me. You're always holding back information. This little hut or whatever this is, is just another example. You didn't tell me about it 'til last week. So, tell me the truth."

There was a severity in her voice that Mimi took seriously. Shannon's mind had always been a rather serious place, and her emotions always close to the edge, but it was clear she meant what she said, even without skimming.

"Alright. What do you want to know?"

"Everything."

Mimi rolled her eyes. "They always do. Just pick something."

Shannon scowled a little. "They? How many women have you brought down to your little hobbit hole?"

Mimi knew from the surface of Shannon's mind that she didn't really want an answer to that question. Few did. She knew that Shannon was a jealous person, but she was feeling a bit annoyed. Plus, the fish hadn't been as good as she had hoped.

She made to count her fingers, pretending like she had to think about it. "Oh... Hmm... I think nine women and eight men have shared this bed."

"Excuse me?"

"What? You told me to be honest."

"So what am I? Your flavor of the month or something?"

Mimi rolled her eyes. "Considering how many years I've been doing this, more like flavor of the decade?"

Shannon's face reddened for a moment and then she smiled. "Ha!" Shannon shouted. "I knew you were older than seventy. Tell me the truth. How old are you? You won't distract me."

Mimi bit her lip. Again, she pretended to count. This time she took much longer to respond even though she knew the exact number. It was hard to forget her 13$^{th}$ birthday. She thought on how easy it is to mark that night as the end of her normal life, to count off the exact distance from it. How could she forget the night she had murdered someone?

"Let's see, in April I'll be 782."

Shannon's jaw dropped, fishlike. Mimi was tempted to throw a piece of fish into it, but restrained herself.

"But... how? Even most Mids rarely live that long with their allotment. Oldest Mid I ever heard of was 650. I mean, Uppers, sure, but they're the only ones who can afford unlimited access to the alcoves."

She shrugged. "You're right. I found an alcove."

"What, just lying around?"

"Yep, just sitting right in the open underground." Mimi knew Shannon didn't understand her sarcasm and heard her ask herself if she was serious. "Yep. Serious."

Shannon's big eyes narrowed, "You're being sarcastic."

It wasn't a question. Shannon was catching on, at least. "It's dangerous."

"So what? So is living on the street for any woman in this city."

"Not like this. My last lover, Daniel... he got..." Mimi froze. She didn't like to talk about Daniel, about what they had done to them. There were worse punishments than becoming a Runner, worse than death. Daniel had been caught red-handed because he hadn't listened to her, had gone to the alcove when she had told him not to.

"Don't even think about it," said Mimi. "It won't happen."

Mimi saw the anger forming in Shannon's mind. She saw what she was about to say. She felt her own rage envelop her.

"Oh, I see. So, every few decades you get yourself a pet, someone to shack up with for a while, someone whom you can cast away when you're bored, when they get too old and you don't want their body anymore."

The anger rolled from Mimi's tongue, like dripping venom. "What the hell do you know? You're just a little girl. Twenty-seven is barely an adult. You have no idea how deeply I've loved. You don't understand what it's like to watch someone you love stolen away from you."

"Um... Tanya," said Shannon.

Mimi felt the anger pulse in her chest. Her heartbeat thudded in her ears. She felt her tone sharpen. "Oh, no, no, no. There are things much worse than becoming a Runner, worse than death. You don't even have a clue." Mimi slammed down the remains of her food to the floor. She stood up at full height, which wasn't much above Shannon's height at sitting. But Shannon drew back.

For a moment, the light of the room tinged red. She had the strange sensation that her words somehow flowed into Shannon's brain almost in the same way that Mimi could skim minds.

"Shannon, I've never had the luxury of watching someone grow old. Every single person I ever brought down here and told my secrets to ignored me. Every single one either left me because I wouldn't tell them how to find the alcove, or ended up a Runner because I did. You have no idea what it's like to live for centuries, having your heart broken over and over again. You have no idea what it's like to lose every single person you love, to have them stripped from you. Wonder why I lie? Because no one ever listens to me, even after I tell them what happened to the others. So, Shannon, I do care about you, or else I wouldn't tell you shit."

Mimi's sight cleared a little, the red tinge faded, but she had not seen Shannon's reaction until that moment. She had not seen the fear and the pain that she had somehow pushed inside her. Shannon sat motionless, eyes wide open. She appeared unable to blink, but tears were pouring down her cheeks. An open faucet.

Then her face came back to life again. She blinked and her cheeks twitched. Shannon's whole body shivered as she buckled from the inside. She was a building, collapsing under its own weight, unable to stop falling.

Mimi reached out to catch her, but missed. Luckily, she fell on the bed.

What had Mimi done to her? Was she able to push her thoughts onto Shannon? Did she somehow... scream into her mind? A sense of panic took her as she examined the ruins and wreckage of the woman she loved. Sharp sobs punctuated the space, deep rasping breaths and gasps for air. Shannon did not seem to be able to speak and Mimi walked closer to her, hesitantly putting a hand on her shoulder.

"Shannon... I..."

Shannon turned over, just enough to look in Mimi's brown eyes. "Did... How... What did you..."

It was all that Shannon could utter.

Mimi felt the anger rise in her again. Shannon had made her do this. It was Shannon's fault and if she didn't get out right that moment, if she didn't get away from her, she would hurt her again. She didn't understand how, but she knew it on some instinctive level.

Her anger was a pulsar, a radical sun, heavy and dense and full of heat and fire. She felt it radiating from her body, felt a desire to scream at Shannon again, to go back to the red. That redness was almost hungry, and now that she had let it see the light of day, it wanted more.

Mimi turned and fled the space. She hurried toward the long metal pipe at the entrance. She didn't know where she was going, but she needed out, needed away.

Why was it they never understood? They always thought she was holding out on them. Didn't they understand that she had loved them all? She watched them all leave, or be taken to the Runnercore or... She swallowed hard. She couldn't let herself think of Daniel. Couldn't think of what he had become. She didn't dare turn her mind that direction.

The red had faded with each footstep. She felt herself cooling. The tectonics of her inner life had settled, for now.

Why did she keep doing it? Why did she keep sneaking into the alcove? Why did she keep extending her years? Most of all, why did she keep taking new lovers? Because she could? Because she needed to fill some emptiness in her? There was some reason, she reached for it, but it seemed impossible to grab hold of.

She heard footsteps behind her, felt the gentle press of Shannon's mind come closer, like an invisible tide gradually rushing in. She did not turn to meet her.

Shannon had come. After what Mimi had done to her, of which she still wasn't sure, Shannon had still come after her.

Her voice was soft and hesitant. "What happened to Daniel?" Shannon waited a moment for a response. "Mimi, please. Tell me. Sometimes it helps if you talk about it. It helped me... no, it saved me to tell you about Tanya. I don't think I could have gone on without telling you. Just tell me. I love you too, you know. I didn't say it earlier, but I do."

Mimi still didn't turn. She kept herself cold, afraid of the return of that redness. "Me. I happened to him." Her voice was cold and quavering. She barely held her tears, her tears cried for freedom. She headed for the surface, breaking for a run, and did not stop until she saw that Shannon wasn't behind her anymore.

# Chapter 3
# Orphan's Alley

MIMI SURFACED AND WALKED the street until she reached the entry to Orphan's Alley. Passing through the mob of homeless, she took inventory of those she recognized and the ones she didn't. They were islands, shackled and disheveled. Some clung to their cart full of possessions, others to the rags that draped their bodies and little else. For most of them, there was little to cling to, and so they clung tight.

Here, the homeless had no fear of the cold winter nights when they may meet endless sleep. They had no hesitation in the heat of the summer sun, needing to seek shade and water to survive the onslaught. They would not starve. They would not die of disease. The alcoves ended disease centuries ago. But some would be beaten; some would be recruited into the Runnercore. Some would be exploited in other ways, especially the women. All were disposable, like so much cast away paper, waiting for a time when their purpose, like so much else in the city, was recycled.

The city had various spaces where the homeless clustered, where they pressed their tired bodies up against ancient brick and mortar. There were only a few places that city security allowed them to live and so there was a limitation to where they could lay their tired heads. This one was called Orphan's Alley. A name that the residents themselves had given it hundreds of years prior. Probably none here were alive to see the naming, but names, like ideas, can be passed on through the generations, and there wasn't much else for the homeless of the city to pass on. Names were their empty legacy.

A single food dispenser had been installed at the end of Orphan's Alley. It provided only the basics, a green algae nutrient-rich soup, once a day. It was enough to keep a person alive, but only just. If you could figure out a way to earn some credits you could get more, but panhandling was strictly forbidden in Manhatsten and so those who the city had cast aside, who it had made orphans, were left with only illegal means. After all, no one would hire you in the city if you did not have a place of residence somewhere. And illegal means usually meant that eventually you were caught and recruited.

Orphan's Alley, a prime recruitment ground.

Mimi found who she was looking for. A man, standing slouched against a corner, thin brown rags covering his body in multicolored clumps held together by safety pins, staples, and in a few places, stitches. He was a tall man with short, dark, greasy hair, chopped off in places with a blade. Facial hair crowded the edges of the scars but did not dare cross it.

His voice was soft and deep. It was a welcoming tone like a snake's slither. "Mimi, good to see you, you know I was just telling the boys you'd be back any day now."

The redness was still there, just under the surface, and Mimi felt it threatening to break free. What part of her had she opened? It was a terrible, empty feeling. It was hungry, and she didn't like it. It almost seemed to be whispering to her, telling her to release it.

Her eyes locked on the dealer. Mimi shrugged. "What else have I got to do to kill the time, Andrew?"

"Hmmm. True enough," a ragged grin spread across his face, revealing several missing teeth. "Do you have credits? Or are you finally going to make some other arrangements?"

"I have credits."

Andrew frowned, "You know, I am sure that if you would like to pay some other way than credits, we could arrange a more physical kind of payment."

"No thanks." She couldn't help but skim his mind. She saw what she didn't want to see. In his mind he was undressing her, peeling back the layers of her ragged clothes, unwrapping her like a little boy's present.

Mimi felt her face flush. The redness rose in her. It spiraled upward. She could almost hear it beckoning her to unleash it on him. It was hungry for him, in the same way Andrew was hungry for her body.

She shook her head. "No."

"Hmmm? What was that, Mimi? Let's make a deal, one night with me for several months' supply of Likatol."

"No, Andrew." She took a step back from him. The redness had died down now, but her normal anger was brewing and she didn't want any more trouble today. Her heart was aching for her argument with Shannon, and she wasn't sure if she could fix it.

"Tell you what, one night and I'll give you a full year's supply. Come on now, that's more than generous, and I certainly won't need an entire night, perhaps just a few hours."

Why was he so insistent? Normally, Andrew knew how to take no for an answer. Mimi risked skimming his mind again for another moment and saw something she had never seen before. Something was pressing on him, putting pressure on him. It was almost like someone was encouraging him, egging him on.

What was happening lately? For so long, she thought she knew the rules, thought that she had everything about her abilities figured out, but first there was that strange silence by her favorite fishing hole, then the redness, and now this? It was almost too much. It was like someone, or something was changing all the rules, and she couldn't act fast enough to figure out what they were.

Mimi shook her head. "No, Andrew." She paused for a moment when his face twitched. Fear traced her spine, a cold finger. She could feel him growing impatient. But this was not the impatience of a man, rather of a stray dog hungry for meat.

She thought about walking away but then her anger released. She wasn't going to be bullied by some low-life dealer. She wasn't going to put up with any of his shit and she was going to make that clear.

She moved up closely to Andrew, leaning in almost as if she was going to kiss him. He leaned in close and then at the last moment, she dug her elbow right into his neck, pressing it into his windpipe. He choked and tried to step back but she had him pinned against the wall. His hands reached up to grasp for her arm but as he did, she pressed harder. His eyes bulged as his skin purpled and she felt satisfaction as she skimmed his mind and found terror.

"Do you really think that I would ever let you put your filthy hands on me, dealer? Do I look like some kind of whore to you?"

He was barely able to draw breath, but he still managed a guttural, gasping, "No."

"Bet you thought I was just some weak little thing, didn't you? You asshole, I've been on the streets longer than you've been alive, and if I even feel your eyes undressing me again, I'll fucking pluck them out and feed them to you."

Mimi thought that despite the dark shade of his face, he paled a bit at that statement, and a quick skim confirmed that not only did he believe her, but that he was thinking, "This bitch is crazy."

"Yes Andrew, I am crazy, and I'm not afraid to maim your ass."

His eyes were beginning to close. She skimmed his mind to wait 'til just before he lost consciousness. She didn't want him to pass out; something might be lost in the experience if he did. She wanted him to remember this day for a good, long while. It wasn't the first time she had to put the hurt on a man like this, and it certainly wouldn't be the last. Her best defense was a reputation and she had to maintain that. Long experience had given her every tool she needed to intimidate even the stronger men.

She pulled back her elbow and he fell forward, taking deep and wide breaths. On all fours, saliva dripped from his mouth as he coughed and sputtered.

Mimi said, "Act like a dog, get treated like one."

There was a moment when his mind was blank, when she was sure he wasn't going to say anything. It passed. At first, he seemed to be having trouble making words, as if he had forgotten language. Then he said, "Forget it, bitch." He wheezed and coughed. "I'm done selling to you."

Mimi shrugged, "Fine by me. I'll take my business elsewhere. You're not the only one 'round here to sell Likatol, asshole. You're just the dumbest and cheapest."

In truth, Mimi hated to have to go looking for another reliable source of Likatol, but she was also tired of Andrew. In the old days, she might have done more than just choke him a little, she might have made sure he remembered the lesson for years to come. But lately, she was getting tired.

"Get the hell away from me, you bitch. I don't ever want to see your face again."

She headed back through the crowd and out of Orphan's Alley. She only had a few days of supply left, so she would have to find someone else soon. She thought she might try one of the other city districts—she preferred staying around District 17 since it was so close to her hovel—but last time she checked, Districts 8 and 13 usually had a steady supply of Likatol.

She walked out past the threshold of the homeless territory, her mind at work on the problem at hand. She had, for the moment, forgotten about Shannon, knowing that the headaches would come soon, that the voices would grow so strong, that tears would come.

She rounded a corner and bumped into someone. The collision caught her by surprise, but a steady hand reached out and grabbed her and kept her from falling. It was Shannon.

Mimi froze. Here was another secret she was going to have to explain, and judging by the look on Shannon's face, she probably had no idea why she could possibly want drugs. And to explain why she needed them, she would have to explain a whole hell of a lot more than her age.

"So, you're a drug addict?" The wrinkles on her forehead creased. Her short blond hair never hid those wrinkles very well.

"No, I'm not."

"So what were you doing talking to Andrew?"

Mimi breathed a heavy sigh. What could she say? That she needed small doses of Likatol to keep the entire city out of her head? That she would get terrible migraines without them because she could read people's minds? Doubtful Shannon would believe her.

"Shannon, maybe it's best if we don't see each other anymore."

Shannon's face changed, from anger and frustration to shock and hurt.

"What? Wait, I don't understand. I..."

"I like my privacy, Shannon. I understand you want to share your life with me, but there are certain things I am not sure I can share, not now anyway. I'm not a drug addict, in fact, what I need is Likatol, but I don't think you would believe me if I told you why I need it."

Strictly speaking, Likatol wasn't a drug, it was a pill that someone could take before going on a drug binge. It would keep the user from losing all control and from becoming addicted, but it wouldn't block the high. Likatol was a kind of drug buffer.

"Try me." There was a note of desperation in her voice. "Please, Mimi, you said you loved me..."

Mimi shook her head. "No, I don't think so. Anyone I have ever told has gotten hurt. It's best if you stay away from me."

Mimi began walking down the city streets. Shannon followed close behind. At first, she kept trying to stop Mimi, to get her to talk to her, but after a while, she just followed in silence. Mimi blocked her out, refused even to skim her. It was better this way. She would give up soon enough, she would go on with her life. Besides, it was better than Shannon leaving her, as some of them did.

After more than twenty blocks, Mimi began to hear sobs and sniffling directly behind her. She tried to ignore it, to let Shannon cry, but after a few more blocks she couldn't take it. She loved her. There was something special about Shannon, something soft and warm. She made Mimi feel safe and warm and special. Shannon really cared about her. It was like, with Shannon, all the wounds from her life on the street didn't ache so much.

She opened herself to Shannon's mind. She dipped into it and there was comfort there. Comfort in knowing that this woman, more than anything, just wanted to feel Mimi in her arms, wanted to embrace her and never let her go. There was something powerful in knowing someone else's thoughts, especially when those thoughts were of love and longing. People said a lot of shit, and their minds so often cast a shadow over the true meaning. But here, here was a woman who truly loved her and knew it.

Mimi could not stand against it. When love comes like that, all you can do is surrender, to lay down your arms and submit to the will of those who would love you. For in denying it, you face only regret. Mimi had been waiting for this a long time, she just hadn't known it.

She stopped. As she turned, she realized that she too had been crying. She looked directly at Shannon, whose streams of tears had eroded the soot in streaks on her narrow face. Mimi reached up and touched her own face, running her finger along her cheeks, her tears had cleansed those parts they had touched.

Shannon stopped and looked at her. She took one step closer and hesitated. Mimi felt Shannon's question press against her. All Shannon wanted was to hold her. Mimi moved closer to her, pulled her close and kissed her. Both minds blanked to the warmth of the embrace. Mimi could taste the salt from her tears on her lips. Then she pulled away slightly and hugged her hard.

"I'm so sorry, Shannon. I love you... I... Let's go back to my place and I'll tell you whatever you want."

Shannon didn't say anything, but skimming her mind told Mimi of the overwhelming relief she was feeling. Shannon's smile was enough. The tears couldn't darken it.

Perhaps it was time to take a chance. Perhaps this time would be for keeps. Maybe that was Mimi's purpose, to love as deeply as she could.

A small voice pushed up in the back of Mimi's mind. "*This one won't last long. It will be even shorter than Daniel. You will watch her suffer. It's what happens every time someone gets close to you. Free her now or you will bring her nothing but misery.*"

The voice almost sounded real, almost sounded external. Mimi felt a bit of a headache and took a few deep breaths.

She looked at Shannon again. She drank in her beautiful eyes and face and raised her right hand up to wipe away her tears. Her heart longed to be with her, to hold her close and feel her touch. She pulled Shannon in close and kissed her again, feeling the warmth of her body pressed against hers, the softness of her lips making her body tremble with joy.

She pulled away, grabbed Shannon's hand and together, they walked home.

# Chapter 4
# An Ancient Past

MIMI LAY NAKED, FEELING the softness of Shannon's skin on hers. Their bodies pressed closer as she pulled a blanket up over them. If she was going to do this, she wanted to feel Shannon close to her, wanted to feel the comfort of her touch. Shannon was much longer than her, but their slender forms accented each other perfectly.

"I'm gonna start at the beginning, if that's okay. I have to warn you, some of this is going to be hard to believe, and I know the fact that I have been hiding a lot of things may not help you believe me, but I swear to you, everything I am about to tell you is the truth, Okay?"

"Okay." Shannon was afraid, but the fact they had just made love had helped ease some of that fear. Mimi hoped her story wouldn't be too much for her, but there was only one way to find out.

"I was born in the third century after the city began its migration. Hard to believe, I know, but my father died in the second uprising after the city began moving. My mother, who became pregnant only days before my father was killed, did her very best to survive in the city alone. She managed to find a job. She had a place to live in the lowers, and began trying to put a life together for me. It was hard. I have a lot of memories of the first years of my life of my mother bringing home security personnel for favors and extra credits."

Shannon frowned. "She sold herself?"

Mimi nodded. "She did what she had to do to survive. And because of it, she was able to get me into a school in the Lower Mids. One of her regulars had a contact there. It was my mother's hope that I could move up into the mids and out of the lowers. The school was even on the 15th level."

"15th? But I thought Lowers needed a special pass to move above ten?"

"Yeah, this guard got me one. I guess he must have really liked my mother. But I can't imagine it was that hard, I mean it's not like he was trying to get access above the 40th level where the Uppers live, right?"

Shannon nodded, "Still, it couldn't have been that easy. Wait, how did you end up homeless?"

Mimi frowned, "I'm getting to that." She shifted her body around and became Shannon's big spoon. Her skin was so soft and warm. She nuzzled Shannon for a moment, then took deep breaths inward, taking in her scent. For the moment at least, she felt safe.

"Things went alright for a while. The mid school was much harder than the lower one, but I'm not stupid, so I did okay. Mostly I pulled average marks. But then my thirteenth birthday rolled around, and everything changed."

"See, I think my mother had become addicted to something. I started to notice changes in her behavior. It was small at first, but after a while, she started to scream at me for not finishing simple chores. A few times she hit me, nothing terrible, mind you, but she did. Before I was twelve, my mother had never raised a hand to me, not once. She had barely ever raised her voice.

Shannon turned to face Mimi again. She was looking directly into her eyes, and Mimi hesitated for a moment and swallowed hard.

"One night, a man came. I don't know exactly who he was, but I figured he was one of my mother's...gentlemen. But then the yelling started. He was yelling about money, that my mother owed him a lot and that her body just wasn't going to cut it anymore. Then he asked where I was, said that maybe I would be able to help her pay the debt."

Shannon's eyes began to water. "No...he didn't."

Mimi shook her head. "Thankfully not. See, my mother, for all her weird mood swings, was not about to let anyone lay a finger on me. So, this man burst into my room and just as he stepped in the door, my mother put a knife right through his back. The man screamed, turned around and began choking her. I jumped up out of bed and began kicking him as hard as I could but nothing would help, he wouldn't let her go. He just kicked me away. He was going to kill her."

Mimi paused for a moment to wipe a tear away from her face. Shannon leaned forward and kissed the spot where the tear had been.

"I did what I had to do. See, the little steak knife was still in his back. I don't think my mother had hurt him very much with it. So, I pulled it out and just started...using it on him. I don't know how many times I stabbed him. I just wanted him to stop hurting my mother." Mimi's voice began to shake, along with her body, and the tears began to flow freely.

"She was all I really had." Mimi buried her face into Shannon's breasts for a moment and sobbed. Shannon stroked her hair in silence until Mimi calmed down.

She sniffled, her voice was low and hoarse. "The next thing I remember is my mother taking the knife out of my hands. I remember her packing my things. I remember her telling me I had to go; I had to hide somewhere. I didn't want to leave, though. I knew what would happen to her if I did."

"Did she...end up a Runner?"

Mimi nodded, "Is there any other punishment in this city?"

Shannon didn't shake her head. She didn't need to. She didn't know there was another kind of punishment, but Mimi didn't feel like it was the right time to talk about it.

"She made me leave though, threw me out the door. Screamed at me, hit me, kicked me, everything she could to get me out the door. She didn't want anything to happen to me. I didn't understand then, and for years after I thought she just wanted to be rid of me, but, well, I've had a lot of time to think about it. I know now that everything she did was to protect me."

Shannon asked, "Then what happened? I mean, how did you end up down here?"

"That's a long story. But there's some other stuff first, like why I need Likatol."

Mimi hesitated. "See, I don't know what it was about that night. I don't know if it was the act of taking someone's life. I don't know if it was my mother kicking me out. I don't know if maybe it had something to do with the fact that I had no idea how to survive on the streets, but something in me woke up."

Shannon cocked her head a little. "What do you mean?"

Mimi looked at her directly in the eyes. "This is going to be hard to believe. But after that night I started to hear voices. At first, I thought I was just going crazy. I thought that maybe I was losing my mind. I noticed that some of the other homeless people talked to themselves and I thought maybe that was where I was headed. But then I noticed something else, that sometimes when I was talking to people, I seemed to hear their voice both when they were speaking and when they weren't. It created a few awkward situations."

Mimi paused for a moment and watched for Shannon's reaction. She deliberately stayed out of Shannon's head. She wasn't sure she wanted to know what she was thinking. Then she saw recognition on Shannon's face.

"Wait...are you telling me...you read minds?"

Mimi looked away from her and nodded. But Shannon grabbed her chin so that she would look directly at her again. Mimi expected her to yell, to laugh, to scoff, or something that all her other lovers had done, but instead she said, "Well shit, that completely makes sense."

Mimi blinked. "It does?"

"Um yeah. You know a lot of shit you shouldn't know. Like when those sanitation workers were coming. You know all this information, that—having dropped out of school—you shouldn't know. I mean I can think of a hundred times when I thought to myself, my god, does she read minds or something? And it turned out to be true."

"So you're not weirded out or mad or anything?"

"No, why would I be? It's just another reason to love you for the amazing person you are."

Mimi's eyes began to burn, and before she could stop herself, she realized she was bawling. Shannon pulled her close. Mimi could feel her fingertips caressing her cheek.

"Why are you crying, Mimi?"

Mimi couldn't answer, she just kept sobbing and pulled herself even closer to Shannon. She wanted nothing more at that moment than to merge with her, to be so intimately close to her that she couldn't ever pull apart again. Here was someone, at last, who might finally be able to understand. And then she felt her eyes closing. For the first time in years, she felt at home.

HER FACE FELT STUCK. She lifted her head and felt the skin between Shannon's bare breasts pull off her face. She blinked and looked around, wondering how long she had been asleep, but there was no way to know. Shannon herself was breathing deeply, her mouth hanging open with her head tilted back.

Mimi ran her fingers up the side of her face. There was so much more to tell her, and for the first time in a very long while, she felt she had a partner, someone to whom she could actually tell things. Of course, it did remain to be seen how Shannon interacted with her now that she knew that whenever she wanted, she could skim her mind. But Mimi wouldn't do that now. Now that she knew, she would respect her privacy. It was a funny thing. It seemed as if the moment someone knew about her abilities, she didn't want to skim them anymore; that somehow, she felt like she was violating some semblance of privacy, yet she had no problem with doing this to a stranger or an acquaintance.

She lifted her body and put her clothes on. They were becoming tattered from wear. She would have to scrape together some more credits for new ones.

She rummaged through a small case to the left of her bed and found her bottle of Likatol. She didn't need much, just a tablet every few days or so. A bottle usually lasted her about six months.

"So, you didn't quite tell me why you need that stuff."

Shannon was sitting up and stretching. She looked around the room, found her clothes around the various locations and put them on.

"Well, it has to do with my...talent, for lack of a better word. See, at first, it wasn't such a big deal. I could easily skim people whenever I wanted."

"Skim?"

"Oh, that's what I call it when I read people. I call it skimming because so far as I know, I can only read what they are actively thinking about. I have never gone any deeper than that, and in truth, with most people, I am a little afraid to do so. People keep a lot of secrets, you know."

Shannon nodded and moved over to Mimi and put her arms around her. They spoke face to face now.

"That's kind of a relief. I can't say I like the idea of you fishing around through my memories and stuff."

"Yeah, and also...I won't read you anymore."

"Huh? What do you mean?"

"Well now that you know what I can do, I don't feel comfortable doing it."

Shannon moved her lips back and forth and looked around the room. "I don't think it's a big deal if you want to read me."

"No, I'm not going to. It's fine."

"Alright. So, the drugs?"

"Yeah, so by the time I turned 16 it started to get more intense. There were these moments when I couldn't control it, and the entire city within a few kilometers would rush into my head. Probably a few hundred thousand people, all speaking at once. It was overwhelming. It made me sick. Sometimes it would just give me a migraine and sometimes it would make me physically ill."

"So the Likatol helps?"

"Yes. I mean, I tried a whole bunch of other stuff first. Lots of people thought I was an addict. But I don't think I was ever addicted to anything. I only ever took something when the headaches were really bad. The problem was, I couldn't stay clear, couldn't function with any of the other stuff."

"Isn't Likatol to stop people from getting addicted to drugs? Like I heard that Uppers would take it before going on a long drug binge or something."

"Yeah, that's what I heard too. And there was one day that my dealer only had Likatol, so I thought what the hell, and gave it a try. I don't know what it is in there, but for some reason, it gives me control over my talent. I don't have to worry about headaches or sickness and obviously, because it doesn't get you high, there are no debilitating effects."

"How often do you have to take it?"

"Thankfully only once every few days, sometimes up to a week. It depends on how stressed out the city is, I think."

"What does that mean?"

"If something stressful is going on, like there are security raids, or there is another migrating city nearby, people get nervous and anxious, and that stress impacts me more. When the city of Lundon did that raid a few years back, and the entire Runnercore went into combat, I had to take two Likatol a day just to keep from getting sick."

"Wow." Shannon kissed her forehead and turned around to gather up her things.

"Going somewhere?" asked Mimi.

"I'm hungry. I thought about getting my daily ration. And see if there is any more news about Tanya. But one thing first, who else knows?"

"No one."

"No one? Not even Bobby or Angela?"

Mimi was mostly a loner, but Bobby and Angela were a couple that she occasionally spent time with. "No, not even them. You have to understand, I can't trust a lot of people with this. If it got out and someone actually believed it..."

"I get it...don't tell anyone, right?"

Mimi nodded. "Please."

"Don't worry, love, your secrets are safe with me."

Mimi watched her leave and head back to the streets. She had the overwhelming feeling that even though Shannon fully intended to keep her secret safe, she wouldn't. She had a sinking feeling that like in times past, everything was about to go wrong. And it seemed like that intuition was never wrong. Perhaps that was a skill set that she had too, that she simply hadn't understood before.

She shivered, closed her eyes, and took a few deep breaths. The cat was out of the bag now and there was nothing to be done. But later, she would think to herself, that there was something she could have done, that when everything went bad, she should have always followed Shannon back up to the surface. She shouldn't have let her leave her side. It might have made all the difference.

# Chapter 5
# Disruption

MIMI COULD COUNT ON one hand the times in her life that she had experienced so much joy.

Over the next few weeks, her days consisted of her and Shannon wandering around the underground of the city, scavenging things to make their home more comfortable. Mimi taught Shannon how to fish. They found new furniture and Shannon spent time decorating while Mimi prepared dinner. New color lined the walls, like the new love beating in their hearts. Their nights were filled with love-making, endless moments of intertwined bodies, giggles and whispers of love. Seas of smiles. Softness.

In the spaces between, they shared stories, shared history, and though Shannon had quickly run out, Mimi could speak for years without pause. After so much time, Mimi felt able to do so again. Her load lightened. Her heart unclenched, and peace was found in so many private corners and corridors in their subterranean space.

Little time was spent on ground level after Mimi had secured a new supplier of Likatol. It hadn't been easy but after several days of searching, she found one they could afford.

The Nowhere became to feel like somewhere. Their somewhere.

There was one subject that Shannon was unable to wrestle loose from Mimi.

"Tell me about Daniel."

Mimi froze. "I don't know if I can yet, Shannon. It's...just so hard to speak of."

The two lovers lay naked and covered in a new bed, scavenged from above. Mimi was warm and safe, but still, it was difficult to speak of.

Shannon stared in Mimi's eyes. Her smile now a likely permanent fixture. "It's okay." She reached up and caressed Mimi's face. "I'm here when you feel ready. I just want you to know the door is open."

Mimi kissed and then nuzzled Shannon. Her face was hot, and one or two tears leaked out. "Thank you. That means a lot."

The room took on a red tinge. Mimi's sense of security evaporated and Daniel's eyes, the white on white on white of where his pupils used to be, became visible. The terror of that pale skin marked with blue lines filled her vision so completely that for a moment she thought she had become blind to all else.

"Mimi?"

Mimi heard Shannon's voice, but it was distant. It echoed and mingled with the normal noises of the underground, the sound fading.

Mimi couldn't move. Daniel's form took shape; a tall figure surrounded by metal. The EnViro suit used to travel outside the city his only garments. The recycled Runners could never leave them. It was their enclosure. Mindless beasts needed an enclosure.

"Mimi, you're scaring me. What's wrong?"

A hug turned into a shake. Gentle at first, then jarring. Mimi's head wobbled. She couldn't move, but she felt her tongue flopping on the inside of her mouth with Shannon's attempts to break the trance. She could hear Shannon in the distance, but all she could see was the form of the undead version of her former lover, colored with a red veil in her sight.

Shannon's voice began to fade away into the distance. Mimi was traveling, and now, what was once Daniel seemed to take notice. She had thought it was just an image, just a memory, but it was more. She was seeing him in real time. It looked at her as if they were occupying the same space. Its white on white on white eyes pierced her. No pupils remained to contract. There was only a blank stare, and she was aware that its mouth was open and that its teeth were no longer human but something much sharper. Blue outlines of veins surrounded the upward tilt of the lips as they formed into a grin. A framed monstrosity.

It moved towards her. Slow steps.

Its hand raised.

Mimi still could not move.

It reached for her throat.

She shivered.

Fingertips brushed skin. A grip taking form.

Then, a sharp pain punctuated her cheek.

She reached up to touch it, to stroke the stinging and found herself still in bed with Shannon. Shannon was screaming her name, was shaking her, weeping and terrified. She drew her arm back to slap Mimi again, and Mimi blinked and put her arm up to stop the motion.

"Mimi? Are you okay? What's happening?" Her voice rough.

Mimi said, "I don't know."

Shannon's eyes widened. "Mimi...did you just..." She trailed off, her face panicked and puzzled.

"Did I just what?"

Shannon's eyes widened again. "Mimi, you aren't opening your mouth when you're speaking."

"What? What are you talking about?"

Shannon slipped out of bed and backed away. "Stop it, Mimi...I don't like this."

"Stop what?"

"Whatever it is you are doing." Shannon began to clutch the sides of her head.

"What am I doing?" She looked down at her hands. Red.

Shannon was backed all the way against the clothed wall. "I think you are in my head. Please stop. Please get out of it. It hurts."

Mimi looked around. She didn't know what to say, what to think. She opened her mouth, but for a moment no words came out. The red tinge was still on everything in the room, it was faint, but it was there. She focused for a moment and imagined that the color wasn't red, that it was blue. She didn't know if that would work, had no idea what was happening, but she had to try something.

Shannon stopped holding her head and looked up at her; she still cowered in the corner, but her expression had changed a little. "There, like that, whatever you are doing, do more of that."

Mimi did. She changed the blue to yellow and then lightened it. Then finally she imagined that there were no colors, that the light was clear.

Shannon relaxed visibly. "What just happened?"

"I don't know, love. I really don't. Nothing like this has ever happened to me before."

Eyes full of worry, Shannon moved a little closer. Was there fear there too? Mimi thought there was. Shannon reached out for her hand.

"Were...were there any other times you lost control of your ability? I mean...after you started taking the Likatol to curb it?"

Mimi thought hard for a moment.

"Yes, there was at least one time, when we were at war with one of the other cities and people were upset."

"What did you do then?"

Mimi thought about it. It had been at least three centuries, maybe four since it happened, but she remembered what it was like. She had thought her head would explode, that someone was taking a power drill and pushing it into her forehead. When one of the buildings had collapsed in the conflict, she heard the screams of those in the rubble pierce through her like an arrow. "I had to find something stronger than Likatol."

"Like what?"

She thought for a moment, then remembered. "Benadixtrin, it was the only thing that would stop it."

"What's that?"

"It's a medicine for treating people with severe schizophrenia."

"What's schizophrenia?"

"It's like when someone hears voices and sometimes they even have trouble understanding if those voices are real or not."

"Like you?"

"No, not exactly, I know mine are real because I can see how people react, but..." Mimi gripped her temples; she was getting a headache. "But I thought it might help, that maybe somehow if it helped them, it would help me?"

"So why don't you take that instead of Likatol?"

Mimi closed her eyes and rubbed her temples. She was finding it difficult to focus. "There were other side effects. It made me sick to my stomach and it was much more expensive. Likatol doesn't have any side effects. I only ever needed Benadixtrin once and haven't thought about it since."

Shannon started to say something then stopped. She moved closer and put her arms around Mimi. "Love, do you think it might be helpful if I go get some for you? Maybe just in case something like this happens again?"

For a moment, Mimi peered into her mind. Shannon was scared of her. Mimi frowned.

"Okay. If that's what you want. I'll keep it around just in case it gets bad again. We can go tomorrow."

"No, that's okay. I can do it now." A quick response.

Mimi looked up at Shannon. She didn't need to skim her to see that Shannon needed some time away, that she needed some space to feel okay with what had just happened. In truth, Mimi needed a little space to clear her head. She had no idea what was happening to her, and maybe a little space would give her a chance to breathe and think about it.

"Alright. Terrance, the short guy on the corner of East 83rd and Madison just by Central Park, he probably has some. He's a tame one too, not like the other dealers, but only usually carries medical-type stuff."

"How much?"

"I don't know, just take what we have left. We can run a few scams on some Mids next week and make up the difference."

Shannon nodded. "How far is 83rd and Madison, you think?"

"It's in District 6, so probably a few hours' walk round trip if you don't take the people mover. You up for that?"

Most of the time they could only get on the people mover for a handful of blocks before ticket checks got them thrown off. Shannon would probably have to walk most of the way at least.

"I think so."

Shannon moved in close, hugged Mimi and kissed her forehead. "I'll be back as quick as I can, love."

Gratitude and relief rose to the surface of Shannon's mind. She was thankful that Mimi didn't argue about her going alone.

Shannon walked towards the flap, lifted it and disappeared behind the cloth. Her footsteps padded away quickly, nearly at a run.

Mimi frowned. That red tinge again? What was that all about? She thought about the afternoon where the workers' minds went silent. Why was all this happening now? It didn't make any sense. After centuries of using her abilities, why would something suddenly change?

Mimi stood and began cleaning up the room. Shannon was a slob. She wasn't much better, but she didn't like to leave too much food lying around. The roaches weren't picky, she'd seen them occasionally, but mostly she had been able to keep them away from her hovel.

Gathering the fish bones, she moved through her cloth door. She walked over to where the uneaten remains of the fish laid and saw a few flies that were curiously probing one of the fish heads. She gathered them up and walked a few dozen paces to where there was a hatch in one of the pipes. She put down the scraps and began to turn the large metal wheel of the hatch. She heard the click of the lock and yanked hard on the door to open it. It squealed and something in Mimi's mind translated that squeal to a scream. It occurred to her that Shannon might not be okay alone on the surface. That maybe she should have gone with her, even if she had made Shannon nervous earlier.

She reached down, picked up the scraps of food and then cast them into the tube that went into the biorecycler. She shut the hatch and again, the squeal made her stomach sink a little. There was a gentle pushing in her mind. Almost like a sense of urgency. Shannon hadn't been gone ten minutes, and she felt a deep desire to check on her.

She went back into the hovel and tried to clean up, but the sensation of checking in on Shannon was growing. She felt instinctively that something was wrong, that she needed to follow immediately. But she denied it. Shannon was already scared enough and needed a moment to herself. Shannon was a big girl. Mimi had seen her talk her way out of trouble a number of times. Shannon was a resourceful woman, it was one of the reasons Mimi liked her.

Mimi sat down on the bed, swung her legs up and laid down. She started to close her eyes and relax. She tried to breathe deeply and let the tension of her muscles be taken by gravity.

The pressure in her mind grew. There was no red tinge this time. But this time the sense of urgency and panic grew in her so sharply that she sat bolt upright, feeling that it was suddenly difficult to breathe. She found herself standing. Found herself looking around for her makeshift spear.

Again, she stopped herself, trying to steady her emotions. Why was she feeling such anxiety?

Then, a voice spoke up. The voice was so clear and so crisp that Mimi was certain that someone was saying it loudly right in her ear.

"Dammit Mimi, forget the spear and just go after Shannon. Her life is in danger."

Mimi's blood ran cold. She didn't know where the voice was coming from and at that moment she didn't care. She did exactly as the voice instructed and before she knew it, she was sprinting toward the pipe that led to the exit.

# Chapter 6
# Paradise Lost

THE STAIRS TO THE SURFACE were agony. Shannon only had to go up and down them a handful of times now, but Mimi walked them as if they were nothing. It seemed to Shannon that Mimi always walked on air. How could a woman bearing such a heavy burden step so lightly?

She opened the door that led out into the surface-level streets. It was still a few hours from designated dark. The city never had darkness anymore, as the giant, glowing shield around it which was fueled largely by the energy of the sun was its own light source. At night, the city was awash in a kind of forever sunset. It was a twilight that twinkled and twirled as the massive legs of the city marched on.

The shield protected them all from the lethal daytime heat and the cold nights. The city, constantly on the move to avoid massive sandstorms, pockets of methane and near-apocalyptic storms on the coast, rumbled almost silently beneath her feet.

Shannon took up the streets. She began walking south toward her destination. It would be a long walk to make it there and back before designated dark, but her recent forays into the underground had built her stamina. Mimi never slowed down, and it was only in the last few days that Shannon finally felt comfortable keeping up.

She walked for several blocks, mind on the earlier events. Had Mimi used her mind to speak directly to her? It had felt strange at first, but then, it had started to hurt. She didn't think that Mimi would ever hurt her intentionally, but if somehow she lost control, Shannon needed something to protect both herself and Mimi. If she could afford it, she would also buy some sort of tranquilizer for a serious emergency. She hadn't decided if she was going to tell Mimi this or not yet, but seeing as Mimi was able to, as she called it, 'skim her mind,' she probably should just tell her.

"There you are."

The voice of the man behind her was familiar. There was an unpleasant tone in the voice. Shivering, she turned slowly. There, standing only a few paces behind her, was Andrew. His face was pale and ragged. Andrew always looked on edge, but there was something more alarming about his demeanor. She couldn't pinpoint it, but her heart made its presence known.

"What do you want Andrew?"

"You."

Shannon blinked, "Me? What did I do? I've never spoken to you in my life."

"I know, it's a damn shame. You know how many conversations I've had with your lover? She never once took the time to introduce us, and we've been business partners for years." His voice was smooth. It only just masked something sinister.

Shannon glanced around to look for a way out, trying not to make it obvious. If he wanted her, it wasn't for anything good.

She measured her will and tried her best to sound calm, but her voice shook just a little. "Oh, it's really okay, I'm not a social person."

Andrew took two steps toward her.

"Oh, but I am. And see, it bothers me a little when I lose a client. I always try to make sure I keep them coming back. Your friend Mimi has been a big source of credits for me over the years, and, call me old-fashioned, but I have a hard time letting go."

Shannon took a few steps back and realized quickly she was against a wall. "So what does this have to do with me?"

"Well, I've seen you two together and I thought, maybe, just maybe, if we sat down and had a chat, that Mimi would decide to resume her purchases, if you know what I mean."

"Well, we're chatting, what do you want me to tell her?" She hoped that all he wanted was a simple chat, but she doubted it. Men like Andrew always wanted more.

"Well, you know, I thought about that. I thought about the fact that Mimi's a pretty tough little girl. I thought perhaps, that it was best if you come stay at my place for a while so she would be...a little more inclined to talk?"

"It's not going to happen, Andrew."

Shannon's heart was racing faster now. She could hear it in her ears, feel it in her forehead. Blood rushing. Fingernails digging in palms.

"But see I think it is, because if you don't come with me right now, well, let's just say I have some connections in security."

Shannon swallowed hard. Ice water filled her veins.

"We can do this the easy way or the hard way. Your choice, Shannon."

Shannon tried to relax visibly. Tried to make it look as if she had resigned. "Alright, I will go with you on one condition."

"What's that?"

"You keep your hands off me."

"Baby, I'll be a gentleman. You got my word."

Shannon started walking, and he walked right alongside her.

"It's not far. When we get there, we'll send someone to find Mimi. I'm sure you'll be out of there in a jiffy. And then you can go back to doing whatever it is you two get up to in the long hours of the night." His grin showed a few extra teeth.

Shannon said nothing. She was watching, waiting for the right moment. She was a smart girl. She had survived on the streets long enough to know that the key to survival is to wait for the right moment to act. She just hoped there would be a right moment. Sometimes there wasn't. Like most street kids, she learned long ago that sometimes there were no options.

Then they walked up East End Avenue. Her eyes traced the wall, only a few yards away, that ringed the edge of the world, the place where the city ended, and the wasteland began. The walls were only about ten feet high, just wide enough to support the shield, itself a semi-physical barrier made of light.

A small hedge grew a little higher than her waist along the road. It was a new thing, something someone had recently planted, but it lined the street. It was a way of trying to mask the wall, to make it less visible, to perhaps hide the view of their world.

Andrew was walking up against the hedge. Shannon glanced around. A thought occurred to her, an opportunity. She marshaled her courage and stopped. Andrew stopped in turn. The small of his back was just above the hedges.

"Why are you stopping, I said it's not far."

"I was just thinking about something."

"What?" His eyes narrowed.

She tried to think of something to say, but nothing came. He cocked his head and chewed the side of his cheek.

"Come on, out with it."

When she didn't respond again, his face darkened. He made to grab her right forearm, but just as he did, she shoved as hard she could. Andrew fell back over the hedge and tumbled. Shannon didn't stay to watch. She ran as fast as she could toward the lower level entrance that led to Mimi's place.

Behind her, she heard angry shouting. She could make out none of it. Her legs pumped hard as she ran down along 79th past Orphan's Ally. When she rounded the final corner that led to the underground access, she slammed right into someone. There was a shout and a muffled cry.

"What the hell are you doing, Lady?"

Shannon, who lay on the ground, saw an arm reach out to her. She took it, and a large man all clad in dark blue helped her up. She brushed herself off and looked up. Her heart sank.

He was security.

She swallowed hard.

Behind them, came a shout. "That's her, Jerry. Hold her." Jerry grabbed her. He was a huge brute of a man with a shaved head and thick black eyebrows. He was well over two meters tall and had a thick, flabby torso. Shannon tried to struggle, but it was no use.

Andrew caught up with them both and stopped. He was panting hard and leaned over, putting his hands on his knees trying to catch his breath.

"Little...bitch...shoved me...right in the damn bushes."

Jerry let out a big hearty laugh. In other circumstances, it might have been a pleasant laugh, but not this one.

"Andrew," he said in his deep, smooth voice, "you didn't tell me how beautiful she was."

"You think she's beautiful, wait 'til you get a look at her girlfriend. They'd both clean up nice."

"Andrew, has anyone ever told you a bird in the hand is better than two in the bush?"

"No, what the hell does that mean."

"It means, I think you should be happy with what you got here and forget the other one."

"Now wait just a sec, that's not the deal we had here."

Jerry's smile turned into a dark scowl. "The deal we have is entirely contingent on what I get out of it. A case of Likatol is nothing compared to the price this one will fetch in the Uppers. I bet you heard of that senator up there, the games she gets up to every night?"

"Reeves?"

"That's the one. Rumor has it, the woman has quite the appetite. I'd be happy to split the proceeds with you, say seventy-thirty?"

For a moment, Shannon was sure that he would say yes and then it would be all over. She would be a plaything for the wealthy. She would never see Mimi again. Her whole world seemed to be crumbling beneath her.

Then Andrew's expression changed. Shannon would swear that he almost seemed an entirely different person. His cheeks turned red. He pulled something out from his rear pocket. It made a loud click. Shannon looked down to see what it was. A switchblade gleamed in his right hand.

"I think you should take the case of Likatol, Jerry. She's mine."

Jerry let out another great, bellowing laugh. Shannon had to admit, the tiny blade didn't look like much of a match for a man the size of Jerry. Jerry pushed Shannon to the ground with her hands behind her back. Her face smashed into the concrete and blood spurted from her nose. With tears forming in her eyes, Shannon turned her body and began trying to stand.

"Now you stay right there, little miss. Uncle Jerry's gonna make sure that we get you to a safe place." Jerry stood a little straighter and sucked in his gut. "Now Andrew, I am gonna give you one more chance to back down. Then, it's off to the Runnercore with you. Is that what you want?"

There was a moment of hesitation in Andrew, and he took one small step back. His thin, wiry body looked like a toy compared to Jerry's. But then, he took one small step forward again and widened his stance.

"You won't be the first member of Security I've killed, Jerry. You don't get to be in the drug trade as long as I have without drawing a little blood from time to time. I've taken down guys bigger and stronger than you. Besides, you aren't allowed to kill me, but I can sure as hell kill you."

Andrew reached into his pocket and popped something in his mouth. Jerry's face darkened.

"What's that," Jerry said taking notice.

"A little something to enhance my strength."

"How did a little shit like you get one of those."

Andrew grinned. Shannon saw a few extra teeth. She shivered.

"I got a few friends in the docks."

"In the Runnercore?"

He nodded.

For the first time, Shannon thought that Jerry looked a little less confident. His jovial smile seemed to melt away.

Shannon watched as the two men began to circle one another. She wished Mimi was here. She had a feeling that Mimi would know exactly what to do. For a moment, she wondered if she could call Mimi, if somehow she could reach out to her. She could read minds, couldn't she? Maybe she could hear her? It was a long shot, but she tried with all her might to call to Mimi, to tell her she needed help.

"You might like that shit in pill form kid, but you'll have wished I killed you when they start you on the chemical injections down below. I've heard it makes even the strongest men scream in agony. I've heard that some of them don't even survive the process. Last chance, Andrew."

Andrew did not waver. He took a swipe at Jerry, but Jerry, despite his size, was far faster than he appeared to be. It was obvious that Andrew had also not expected this, and Shannon watched his eyes grow wide.

While both men were distracted, she tried to stand and was amazed how hard it was without the use of your hands. She laid back down, rolled over on her stomach and then lifted herself up onto her knees. She got to her feet and took a single step forward.

"I don't think so, little lady," Jerry said. With one quick swipe, he knocked her right back down and she landed on her face. This time, she felt a tooth pop and tasted blood. She started sobbing but turned to watch the fight. She almost wished Andrew would win. If he really wanted to deal with Mimi, it was a lot better than becoming a plaything of one of the wealthy up in the tops of the skyscrapers.

At the moment that Jerry had turned to knock her down, Andrew had taken a quick swipe at Jerry's mid-section. He had scored a minor hit; a dark patch was beginning to spread on his uniform. Unfortunately for Andrew, he didn't even seem to notice.

Nor was Andrew's retreat quick enough. Though he had sliced Jerry, Jerry had turned around and smashed his fist right into the side of Andrew's face. The momentum of Jerry turning had given the punch extra weight, and Andrew was knocked down by that singular hard blow.

Jerry pulled his foot back and went to kick Andrew in the gut, but Andrew rolled out of the way just in time and got back on his feet. The left side of his face was already swelling up.

Footsteps slapped the pavement hard from behind Shannon. She hoped to god it was Mimi, but it sounded like several people. Maybe she would have the chance to get away with other people interfering. She rolled onto her stomach again and waited. She would bolt the second Andrew and Jerry were distracted by the newcomers.

She felt a hand grasp hers and lift her. They were big, strong hands.

"What the hell is going on here, Jerry?"

Shannon was standing upright now but was held firm by a medium-sized security officer. His light eyes and thick mustache both twitched as he examined the scene.

"Capitan Richardson, oh man. Glad you're here."

Shannon distinctly noticed a tone in Jerry's voice that suggested otherwise and the captain seemed to notice it too.

"I bet you are, Jerry. You better explain just what in the hell is going on here."

"This lady here, seems she's been trading sex for drugs, and I think this guy is her dealer. I overheard them and intervened."

To her surprise, the captain seemed to doubt this story.

"I bet, Jerry. You and I need to have a long talk when we get back to the station. Maybe it's even time you and Daniels had a chat."

Jerry stopped dead in his tracks. He turned his entire body away from Andrew and Andrew broke to run.

Jerry heard the footfalls and turned. "Hey, shithead, get back here." Before the captain could say another word, Jerry began his pursuit. Shannon saw her chance as the captain was distracted and ran the opposite direction.

Neither of them got very far. Jerry tackled Andrew quickly, and the captain grabbed Shannon before she made it fifty feet. The handcuffs made running odd.

Captain Richardson said, "Look, I don't know what's going on here, but I can't just let you run away from one of my SOs. Looks bad. We'll bring you in and try to get to the bottom of this.

Shannon's face fell.

MIMI HAD WATCHED THE whole thing. She watched as the guards took Andrew and Shannon away. How could this have happened? She took a deep breath. There was no time to worry about that now. She had to think quickly. Would there be a way to free Shannon from the SOs? She didn't know.

She tailed them for many blocks from the shadows of the alleys. She knew the streets well. Every crack was familiar. Every shadowy spot was an ally.

There were no openings. No gods or devils intervened. Why would they, they were from nowhere. Even the gods and the devils cared little for those from nowhere.

When Mimi watched Shannon cross the threshold of the entrance to central security, hope leaked from her heart like a barrel of water with a hole in it.

The giant migrating city of Manhatsten had a rigid legal code. No lawyers. No public defenders. Only favoritism. Mimi had seen it dozens of times. History is a circle.

She found a place to weep, to sag in the concrete. A corner of shadows. Stinging tears. Smoky vision. Utter despair. Sleep.

SHE WAS BEING LIFTED. Dreaming? No. The smells were too strong. She started to struggle.

"Easy now. Calm yourself." The woman's voice was soft and soothing. A strange calm fell over Mimi.

Her voice embodied a dreamlike quality. "Where are we going?"

"To a library. You will be safe there."

Mimi was certain she would be. Rarely had she been so certain of anything in her life. She found that she did not mind letting the two large SOs carry her. She didn't mind much of anything.

This concerned her. Like the tumbling of a lock, things began to click in her mind. She became unsettled again, felt the urge to resist, to lash out, rising.

"Calm, Mimi. I am not your enemy." The voice was compelling.

Another's woman's voice said, "Damn. She broke through already?"

Mimi couldn't see either of them. Both them walked in front of the two SOs who carried her. One had long blonde hair, the other a fiery red.

"Yes, it's curious how quickly she bypassed my suggestion."

"She's dangerous. We should put her back where we found her."

"Ryla said the same thing about you when we found you."

"Maybe, but at least I had an honest job. This one is like a stray cat."

"Feral cat. And I would hardly call Running an honest job."

"Either way Noatla, I don't know if she can be trusted."

Mimi listened, and her agitation began to grow again.

"Rest, Mimi. Soon you will have answers."

"How many times do you think you are going to have to do that?"

"At this rate, a half dozen more."

"Can't we make these SOs go any faster?"

"Serah, you know very well what will happen if we push too hard. Besides, what's the rush? Soothing her isn't so difficult. It's also clear she doesn't know the full extent of what she can do."

"How can you be sure of that?"

"If she knew what she was capable of, do you think she would have allowed her lover to be taken away like that?"

"I guess you're right. Maybe we should suggest that she sleeps again?"

"Mimi, are you tired?"

Mimi knew it was the woman with the blonde hair speaking, but she did not turn to face her. She had the strangest impression that this woman was not using her lips to speak.

Mimi said, "I...I don't think so." The moment the words came out, she realized that she wasn't using her lips, either.

"Mimi, I think you're tired. I don't even know how you can keep your eyes open. Why don't you just rest a while? I bet it would feel wonderful to close your eyes, just for a few minutes."

"But Shannon...I have to..."

"Shannon can wait. We will make sure she's okay. Just close your eyes, Mimi. You know how good it will feel, how easy it is just to let your eyelids close. After all, they're so heavy."

"No. I can't..."

Mimi forced her eyes to stay open. She felt the agitation rising in her again. She felt the strength in her arms and legs returning.

"It's not working Noatla. You better do something fast."

Noatla said, "Officers, put her down gently. I want to speak with her."

They obeyed. Mimi jumped up, ready to run, but Noatla, a tall, thin, blonde woman, grabbed her by the arm and held her tight. She was surprisingly strong for how skinny she was. Her face appeared to be chiseled from rock, and her light eyes were piercing.

"Wait a moment, Mimi, just listen."

Mimi had been wrong. The woman's lips moved just like anyone else's. Perhaps she was mistaken because of what she had done earlier in the day?

"Why should I?"

"You want to help Shannon, don't you?"

"Yes."

"You'd think after all the resistance she put up when we tried to get her up here earlier, that she didn't want to save her girlfriend," The red-haired woman said.

"Hush, you know all too well what it was like before you entered the Order. Mimi, do you recognize me?" asked Noatla.

"No, should I?"

Serah said, "Of course she doesn't recognize you, you think this one votes?"

Mimi said, "Votes?"

Noatla smiled. Mimi liked her smile. She began to notice how attractive this woman was. A pang of guilt hit her chest, and her mind turned back to Shannon.

"Yes Mimi, I am Senator Noatla Lightfoot of District 14. This district. If you come with me, I might be able to help you with Shannon."

Mimi scowled. "Why would you want to help me and why should I believe you?"

"Those are both very good questions. All I ask is that you come with me to the library and hear me out. After that, you are free to do whatever you wish."

"With the SOs following us? How do I know you don't want to sell me to one of your Upper friends?"

Noatla frowned for a moment, but then stood and turned to face the SOs. She said, "You may go now. You are needed in District 13."

The two SOs turned and left without a moment's hesitation. Mimi felt a deep sense of relief to see them go, but she still was wary of trusting an Upper. The Uppers loved to mess with the homeless, some of them got off on it.

Serah said, "What's in District 13?"

Noatla smiled, "Oh, probably nothing, but I am sure they will figure out something *important* to do." Noatla turned back towards Mimi. "So, will you come with us?"

This time, the woman wasn't using her voice. Her lips were still. Then it occurred to Mimi.

"Are you like me? Can you skim?"

Noatla smiled. "Much more than just, as you put it, skim."

Mimi asked, "What's at the library?"

"A chance for you to use your gifts for the benefit of this city. A chance for you to be off the streets and in a safe home."

"Why? What's in it for you?"

"Come, listen. Hear what we have to say. I promise if you choose to leave, no one will stop you. As you've already seen, we cannot even pacify you for long. You have an extraordinarily strong mind."

Mimi nodded and followed.

# Chapter 7
# A Hidden World

MIMI DIDN'T KNOW WHAT to think. A whole room filled with other women, women with her same abilities. All sixteen were sitting in a semi-circle, in a lower level of an ancient library. Here, there were still semi-preserved books in paper. Mimi couldn't fathom just how long some of these books had been around.

There was, however, a much more important question. How was it that she had gone so long living in the city without knowing about this strange little club?

Noatla said, "Actually, the more pertinent question is, how did our Order go so long without stumbling upon you? It's a mystery to us."

Mimi almost spoke up, almost said something about it feeling like a violation, having your mind invaded. Instead, she laughed. Being on the other side of it was strange. Daniel had made a similar comment once, that it felt invasive to have your mind probed all the time. Which was one of the reasons she had decided to stop doing it to those who knew of her ability.

Noatla said, "You'll learn how to think without thinking on the surface of your mind soon enough. Every one of our sisters here has learned this skill."

Mimi said, "Why, so you can keep secrets from each other?"

Noatla shook her head. "No, it's more about allowing yourself time to think and reflect before you say something. Except, here we don't have the barrier of thought to spoken language." Mimi noticed that Noatla was no longer using her lips to speak and that all of the other women seemed to be nodding in agreement.

Mimi chose to speak out loud. "What makes you think I want to stick around? That I want to join your little club?"

The woman with red hair she had met on the street spoke in mind-to-mind contact with Mimi, "Because we have a chance to actually free your partner."

"Mimi, this is Serah," said Noatla. "Serah is a Runner."

Mimi's eyes widened. "Impossible."

Noatla shook her head, "No, not impossible. Not if you allow us to teach you some of the other things you are capable of."

"And just what is it that I am capable of? Mind control?"

"No, not control," said Noatla. "Mind suggestion. We cannot control anyone's mind, but we can give them suggestions. If they are things they are already inclined to do, then they are easy to motivate. If they are things they are resistant toward, it takes a little more skill to get them to comply. It really isn't much different from conversation."

"And if they don't comply?"

"Then we seek another route."

"Why not simply try to force them?"

Several of the sisters eyed each other. It was a long moment before Noatla responded.

"Because trying to force a mind can have terrible consequences."

"What kind of consequences?"

For a moment, Mimi thought that Noatla was going to answer.

"No, Mimi, this is not the time for such a conversation. But let me say that it is dangerous to both the giver and receiver of the orders, and so it is one of the things we consider taboo in this order."

"Fine. So, you said you could help me. What's the catch?"

This time it was Serah who answered. "Membership."

"Membership?"

Noatla nodded, "Yes, we want you to join the Order of the Eye, to complete our circle."

"Creepy name for a women's club."

This solicited laughter from a few of the other women in the room, even Noatla chuckled a little.

Noatla said, "True, I suppose without context you might think it is a strange name. But the title clarifies what we are. Besides, I didn't choose it."

"And what are you?"

"Watchers, mostly. We try to interfere as little as possible in the affairs of the city. But we do watch and protect the city."

"Protect it from what?"

Noatla considered, but this time only for a moment. "Again, in time."

Mimi shrugged and ran her fingers through her black hair. "Have it your way. So you want me to join your little club and then Shannon goes free? What happens to me after that? What happens to her?"

"Well first, as a senator, I am hoping that I can use some of my connections to prevent her from ever even going to a trial. If I can manage to do that, then any further intervention will be unnecessary."

"And then?"

"Well, we would like you to join the Order of the Eye. But we, of course, cannot force you to remain among us, nor would we want to. If you wish, you can disappear into that interesting little hovel you have down in the lower levels."

Mimi eyed Noatla and then looked around the room and saw, with certainty, that all these women knew where she lived.

Mimi shrugged. "Alright, you know where I live, how long have you known and how the hell did you find out?"

"Actually, we only found out a few weeks ago. That afternoon when you encountered the sanitation workers. You tried to push on them, to force your way into their minds. That alerted Sister Kayla to your presence. Before that, we were ignorant of your existence. After that, we had you followed."

"You could read that from here?"

"To try and control someone or to try and force open their mind so you can read their deeper thoughts requires a massive expenditure of energy. There are only two places you can draw that energy from: yourself, in which case you could make yourself very ill, or from something else alive around you. If there is a great deal of life around you, then the cost to those living beings is low, they may feel a sense of weakness temporarily and nothing more. But that impact would ripple outward. The stronger the push, the more energy it would expend and the further out it would spread. So, when you tried to push your way into those two individuals' brains, it sent out a kind of shockwave through part of the lower levels of the city. Sister Kayla, here, happened to be residing in that area for a few days while she was working on a project for the Order. She recognized the feeling and then waited 'til you came the surface. After we felt out your mind specifically, it was easy to find you, wherever you went."

Mimi shifted uneasily. "How were you able to pick me out, out of so many people?"

"Training, mostly. This skill is like any other tool. It can be trained and developed for particular purposes. Of course, you will have to give up Likatol in the long run, but we can take our time weaning you off it."

Mimi frowned; they seemed to know everything about her.

"Some of our sisters have certain specialties, certain skills they can focus on and develop more keenly than others, just like with any skill set."

"So, Sister Kayla," Mimi noticed the woman with short gray hair sitting in the corner, "can detect people who have our particular kind of talents?"

"That is one of her specialties, yes. We can all do it if the person is close enough, but Sister Kayla can reach anywhere in the city. She has the greatest range of any of us."

Mimi reached up and brushed the hair out of her eyes. She wondered what Shannon was doing at that exact moment. But her thought trailed off back into her present circumstance. Then it occurred to her, and a grin spread across Noatla's face.

Noatla said, "Yes, my particular focus is to soothe people. I have always had the ability to help others feel less stressed and to disarm them when they put up emotional barriers. I can sometimes make them feel a bit more tired, so it acts as a tranquilizer."

"Then stop. I don't want to be soothed."

Noatla nodded, but her face betrayed concern. "Very well, if that's what you want. Please understand I only wanted to help you think a bit more clearly, rather than running off and trying to solve the situation yourself."

"So if I join your little club, you'll help me prevent Shannon from becoming a Runner?"

"That is the hope, yes."

"What if you can't? What if she becomes a Runner and you can't stop it?"

Serah spoke up. "Then our task becomes much harder, but not impossible." Serah was using her voice, not directly communicating with her mind. "See, every time someone becomes a Runner, they go through a series of procedures. But the very first one is an implant in the base of the skull."

"What does that do?" asked Mimi.

"It is a behavior chip. If you do something that's threatening or disobey your orders, they send a significant shock to your system. It's not one that is strong enough to kill usually, unless they turn up the voltage, but it keeps you incapacitated for a decent amount of time.

Mimi shifted in her chair and looked again around the room at all the faces that were staring at her. All the eyes pierced her, but in a strange sense, this did not unsettle her, not even a little bit. It occurred to her that she likely had the same piercing eyes. Shannon and all those partners before her had often complained of the way she stared at people. Perhaps she would fit in here. And perhaps these women could offer her a way to become even more powerful and knowledgeable. Maybe she would have enough knowledge to protect anyone she loved.

"Alright, what do I have to do to sign up?"

Serah said, "Just like that?"

Mimi shrugged. "Seems like I have a lot to gain and not much to lose. You already know where I live, you're clearly more powerful than I am, and if you want can make me do what you want me to do. And, you can read what I am thinking, so you know that the idea of having access to more power sounds good to me. I've lived on the streets long enough to know that you take what you can get."

Noatla frowned. "I am not sure I would put it the way that you did, but I am glad you are interested."

Mimi looked directly at Noatla and used her mouth to speak. "No offense lady, but you're an Upper, those rich people up at the top of the skyscrapers, none of you have a clue what it's like to live on the streets. Even those of you who are in the lowers don't have a clue what it's like. You know what it means when you're from nowhere? When you are a person without a home in this city?"

She paused and looked around. No one answered.

"It means that you're disposable, that you're just another bag of skin waiting to waste away. Most nowhere women have been sexually assaulted by security guards. Shannon and I, we're one of the lucky few. Why are so many women assaulted? Because those assholes can do whatever they want to us without consequence. And for the men? Well, some of the SOs prefer men and the others, they get to be punching bags, objects of ridicule and scorn. They blame us for being homeless, but they don't know our stories. They assume we're lazy, we're trash, we're just an unpleasant smell or an eyesore on the street. We're deviants to be ignored. But I'll tell you what, I've been around longer than most of you've been alive, and the one thing I know is that being from nowhere never changes."

"And just how long have you been around," asked a woman in the corner, "that you grace us with so much wisdom?" A squat blond woman sat in the corner. She didn't use her mouth to speak, but Mimi was starting to get the hang of being able to figure out who was speaking. There was a kind of tugging in that direction whenever they did. Mimi specifically kept the number of her age out of her mind.

"A few centuries."

A round of mental murmurs went around the room.

The woman spoke again, "That's not possible."

"But it is, Fatima," said Noatla. "Don't you see what her specialty is?"

The woman Noatla had called Fatima shook her head.

"It took me thinking about it these last few weeks Fatima, but I think I finally understand. Mimi, can you...skim...as you put it, me for a moment and tell me what you see?"

It was a strange request. One that Mimi had never been asked to do before. But, she thought it worth a shot. There was a lot of shit in this woman's brain. All kinds of schematics and fancy words. The woman was a regular library. But, Mimi assumed that she wanted her to see something specific, so Mimi focused a bit until she had something.

"You want me to repeat it back to you, or?"

"Yes, please."

"You were thinking about an archaeological dig. Particularly one where the city of Boston used to be. You were thinking about the layers of sites on top of sites and how the indigenous occupants left a great deal of archaeological data down below the surface of the colonial town, and that in turn was covered by concrete again and again between the 20th and 21st century."

Noatla's smile widened. "No Mimi, I wasn't thinking of anything. I was blocking you. Do you see what she has, Sisters? Why she could survive so long in this city?"

There was silence as all fifteen of the other women were listening.

"Mimi, you have something that we've never encountered before. The innate ability to pull subconscious information from someone's mind. I was thinking about that site a few days ago, but I had put it in the back of my mind to hold on for later after we are finished assisting you. But it seems that you, Mimi, are able to pluck scientific data right from me, without my directly thinking about it."

"I am?"

"You found one of the private access alcoves in the underground, didn't you?"

Mimi nodded. "Yeah, some guy came by one day, he was an engineer or something I think, and he was thinking about its location."

"I actually doubt he was. It's more likely that you were simply mining his subconscious for the information you wanted without realizing it."

Mimi thought about that. It did make a certain kind of sense. Some of the workers she had encountered had always seemed to be thinking of very technical things, and for a little while she had thought it odd, but eventually she had gotten used to the idea that some people just thought that way. She realized her impression was that everyone was thinking that way. Now she knew why she could understand the systems surrounding the algae cultivation, or how she had learned how to hack a food dispenser with ease.

"Yes Mimi, all that and more."

Mimi looked up at Noatla specifically and realized the woman was grinning ear to ear. She was like a kid in a candy store with the keys after hours. Mimi wasn't sure how she felt about that.

"So, I'm accessing people's deepest thoughts without them realizing it? Isn't that what you said you couldn't do? That you can only take stuff off the surface?"

Noatla's eyes drifted up and to the left. Her face went blank for a moment. "Tell me, Mimi, when you have accessed this information, is it only ever information pertaining to technology or science? Or do gleam other kinds of information?"

Mimi thought about it hard for a moment. Sure, she could hear what people were directly thinking about, but most of the time that didn't contain the kind of deep technical information that she had access to. She tried to remember an example of something that she had been given that would be considered a dark secret or gossip, but she couldn't come up with anything off the top of her head.

"Honestly? I'm not sure. Maybe now that I am paying attention I could tell you, but right now I don't think so."

Noatla nodded. "I think you will find that you are only able to grasp certain kinds of information. I am unsure at the moment what the pattern of this information is. It may be that you can only grab onto scientific data. Or it maybe it has something to do with a particular part of the brain's memory connections that you are accessing. But obviously, you have a specific skill set, one that we haven't come across before now. It is one that could be powerful and useful."

"What do you mean? It certainly helped me survive this long, but how could it be of use to you?"

"Can you think of no reason we might want technical information?"

Mimi considered. "I don't know."

"Mimi," said Noatla, "I want you to take a read on Serah."

Mimi couldn't help but notice Serah's face change. It almost darkened.

Serah said, "Why me? I don't want her poking around in the depths of my mind."

Noatla said, "I am reasonably certain that she isn't going to be fishing around through anything personal, but I am curious what information she could glean from you. Of course, I would like your consent just in case, Serah."

Serah grimaced a little and shook her head, but then said, "Fine. Go ahead."

Noatla nodded in Mimi's direction. "Go on, Mimi."

Mimi did as she was instructed. She closed her eyes this time and pictured Serah. At first, there was nothing, just the blank of being blocked from the surface of her mind. Then tiny rivulets of memories began to stream forward, like a trickle of water penetrating into deeper crevices of the earth. Then, there was an explosion of information and Mimi opened her mouth and let some of it drift out.

"Runner protocol 3. The EnViro suit is your best friend out in the Barrens. It will keep you alive through the various sandstorms, methane pockets, and enemy attacks. There are two kinds of EnViro suits, Recon-grade and Battle-grade. The Recon-grade EnViro suit is lighter and more mobile and usually does not carry weapons. In place, it is primarily equipped for surveillance. The Battle-grade EnViro suit is equipped for city to city combat. This suit is equipped with a variety of weapons that are often measured for the aptitude of the user. Some may carry heavier artillery-style weapons, while others may carry short-range laser or projectile weapons. At the same time, some Runners, such as Runner 17, may carry multiple classes of weapons as he, in particular, is skilled in a variety of weapons, including blades and hand-to-hand combat."

Mimi stopped for a moment and looked around. "Should I go on?"

She noticed Serah's eyes, wide and shocked. "Holy shit. That sounded like the recording I heard when I was going through Runner orientation decades ago."

Noatla nodded. "Exactly. It appears to be that Mimi can glean some important part of long-term memory associated with technical information. It will be interesting to find out what your limits are."

"Find out what my limits are? You make it sound like I'm already on board."

"Aren't you, though?"

Mimi obviously couldn't hide what she was thinking, at least not yet. She thought then that it was best to be candid.

She shrugged. "I'm a practical woman. I know that I'm at your mercy and I'm willing to go along with it so long as there is something in it for me. But that doesn't mean I have to like you or even trust you."

Noatla frowned. "I'd rather you not think of it like that. I hope in the future you will learn to love us and call us your sisters."

"Maybe. But I've been around for a while. I'm keenly aware that this world is pretty damn merciless. Who knows, maybe tomorrow another city will kill us all and it won't matter."

A sea of frowns. Only one face with a smile.

"But yeah, I'm in."

# Chapter 8
# An Initiation

THERE WAS LITTLE PREPARATION for what took place next. The Order of the Eye had a rather strange initiation, and Mimi was part of a circle. The lights were dimmed. The seventeen women stood hand in hand. Noatla took Mimi's hand to her right and another woman reached out and grabbed her hand on her left.

In chorus, the voices united. "Welcome, our new Sister."

No lips moved.

One at a time, the sisters introduced themselves.

Immediately to Mimi's left, a woman said, "I am Darla of the Lowers. Welcome."

"I am Rachel of the Mids. Welcome."

"I am Serah of the Runners. Welcome."

"I am Lucy of the Lowers. Welcome."

"I am Fatima of the Uppers. Welcome."

"I am Vala of the Mids. Welcome."

Mimi was noticing a pattern. All of them seemed to have a place where they were from, even Serah, who likely had the most difficult life. But where would Mimi say she was from? She had her hovel underground, but was underground a place you could call home? Would she even call her little hovel of tied-together cloth a home? She wasn't so sure.

"I am Rebecca of the Uppers. Welcome."

"I am Joan of the Lowers. Welcome."

"I am Shandie of the Lowers. Welcome."

"I am Kayla of the Mids. Welcome."

"I am Leahara of the Lowers. Welcome."

It also occurred to Mimi that so many of them seemed as if they were from the Lowers. Why was that? Mimi realized that she still had no idea why she was able to reach into other people's minds. Why were any of these women able to do it? Was it some ancient genetic thing? Why weren't there any men? Was that by design or was it impossible for men to have this particular skill set? She felt the questions burn in her and she was just about to open her mouth to speak, when Noatla squeezed her hand and looked her directly in the eyes. There were no words, but Mimi understood its meaning. Not now.

"I am Rosita of the Lowers. Welcome."

"I am Lana of the Mids. Welcome."

"I am Yoshi of the Uppers. Welcome."

"I am Patricia of the Lowers. Welcome."

The circle came around and the final voice spoke in her mind. "I am Noatla of the Uppers, standing Matron of the Order of the Eye, and I welcome you, Mimi."

All eyes were on Mimi. They were waiting for her to speak. But what could she say? She was Mimi from...well...she was from Nowhere. Maybe that was the point. Maybe somehow, being from Nowhere was important. She decided not to shy away from it. She had seen more of this city than most of the others combined. She had traced its underbelly and tasted its corruption.

She shrugged. "And...I am Mimi of the Nowhere."

Curious looks. A pause. Then, acceptance.

The women spoke as one. "Welcome, Mimi of the Nowhere."

Noatla spoke, lips still stationary. "What do you ask of us, Mimi of the Nowhere?"

Mimi looked around at the faces of the women. "To...join you?"

Noatla nodded her assent and smiled. "As you wish. Are there any here who would oppose Mimi's induction into the Sisterhood of the Order of the Eye?"

Silence.

Serah of the Runners departed from the circle, returning only a moment later with some kind of chalice in her hands. They passed the cup. Small sips for each woman's lips. The cup reached Mimi's hand.

"What's in it?"

Noatla smiled. "Your path forward."

Mimi eyed the cup. "That's not an answer. I won't drink it unless you tell me."

Serah said, "If you want in, you drink."

Mimi's head turned towards her, "Then take your cup back." And she held it out towards Serah.

Noatla intervened. "It's a mild hallucinogen, Mimi. It won't hurt you. It is meant only to help guide you toward your role in the Order. It is important for you to begin your first steps among us."

Mimi had, in fact, tried many kinds of drugs over the years. She hadn't cared for most, but hallucinogens were usually fairly benign. She considered that each of the other women had taken a small sip and imagined that a small sip probably couldn't do very much to you. So, she tilted the cup up and took a tiny sip.

Serah spoke, "No, all of it."

With a stern voice that Mimi would have never expected from her, Noatla said, "Who is Matron here, Serah? Do not speak out of turn again." She looked at Mimi. Her voice softened. "You must drink the remainder, dear."

Mimi let her eyes move back and forth across Noatla's face and then without breaking her gaze, downed the rest of the cup.

Serah walked over and took the cup. She glanced at Mimi. She was all iron eyes.

All the sisters sat, and Mimi followed suit.

A call and response began.

"The eyes come open," said one sister.

"The sleeper wakes," said another.

The voices shifted with each call, as if the room was echoing itself. Mimi could not trace the voices as they spoke. They began to blur together.

"The wheel turns,"

"As Above,"

"So Below,"

"As Within,"

"So Without,"

"The Light passes and time squints, allowing the faintest glimmer of wisdom."

"But Fear is the little death, the one that brings an end to hope,"

"Fearlessness is the key that unlocks all things."

"You will die."

"We will all die."

"Rest in these words."

"Rest in body,"

"Rest in Mind."

The word Mind became long and strung out. It echoed and repeated, over and over again, and the light in the room became total whiteness, stealing colors. Blending, abducting, rearranging so that the room was a smokescreen of objects and stole their form and figures. Then there was only white, and then that faded too, until all was transparent and clear but empty and pregnant.

She looked around. There was no she to look. No hands to find, no body to fill the space. Just a watcher. Then she thought of Shannon and Shannon appeared. She was huddled in the corner of a room, crying. This made Mimi think of her mother, of that terrible night. As she thought on this, the body of the man she had stabbed many times appeared on a fragment of floor in the empty space. The blood spread from underneath his corpse.

Anything Mimi thought of appeared and took weight into reality. But she wasn't sure where or why she was here. She remembered standing in that musty old library, but how did she jump from there to here? She remembered the cup, and she knew she was tripping.

Yet there was something else about this place that warranted examination. If she could think of something and make it appear, could she do that with something from the future as well?

She thought on Shannon, and she appeared, standing before her. Mimi turned her mind to Shannon's abduction and in the corner of the space, the scene replayed itself over and over. She had a grip on the past. Could she reach into the future? She tried to think of Shannon in the future, but nothing came.

So why was she here, then? If she couldn't do anything besides look at the past, what value was there to this little ritual?

Momentarily, the scene tinged red. A shadow of red that extended over all. She felt chills and discomfort despite not having a body, but just as the ice seemed to climb firmly up her spine, the red shadow passed on and the light was clear once more.

"Why I am here?" Her words echoed through the space, despite not having vocal cords. She didn't expect an answer; it was more of something to say to fill the time.

"To become better than you are." An image of her mother stepped in from nowhere. Her mother, still young and full of life and kindness, stared at her, and Mimi found that she once again had a body, but it was the body of a much younger version of her, one that had just turned 13.

"I don't understand."

"The Order found you. Now you have the chance to become something more than you are. No longer do you have to be from nowhere. You can have a home again."

"Sure, until that home is taken from me all over again."

"It is true that nothing lasts forever, but the connections we make now have the chance to transform us. When you embrace your sisters, you will become your sisters."

"What is that, some kind of philosophical bullshit?"

The form that was her mother chuckled. "You always were straight to the point, my Mimi. But I think you will find that the people we choose to love shape us more deeply than we can know. Why do you think it's so hard when they depart? It is as if the shape that had help craft in us was suddenly and violently plucked out."

"So what is it you want from me?"

"To remember friendship. To remember community, to remember that even though you may have made some poor choices in the past, every moment of every day is a chance to sew new seeds for a brighter future."

"Again, more philosophical bullshit. I've lived on the streets too long to buy into any of that garbage. You know what changes on the streets? Nothing except the players playing their parts. The streets are always the same, always full of people who will hurt you for a few credits."

"That is true, to a point. But even in the darkest of places there are always those who shine like lanterns, who bring warmth and love and light to those around them. They are a refuge, a shelter from the storm."

"Like who?"

"Like the sisters who have opened their world to you. In each of the places they are from, Lowers, Mids, Uppers, or Runners, they bring light to those around them. They do their best to encourage love and justice."

Mimi considered. "So what, I'm supposed to be a light to the people on the street? A light to the Nowhere?"

"It is one of your options."

The woman's form flickered.

"Who are you, really?"

The woman acted as if she didn't hear Mimi.

"You have many paths you can choose to take now. You can trust your new sisters and walk with them into the future. You could take their knowledge and then abandon them, or you could turn back and go the way you came."

"Why would I want to stick around these women? What could they possibly do for me?"

"They can love you. They can give you purpose."

"And if I decide to either take their knowledge and run or go my own way?"

"That direction will lead you to continue your lonely life. Why would you want to continue that? We both know that you wonder why you persist, for what purpose you continue on. You have lived for centuries, and you have little to show for it."

Mimi felt herself squirm. The woman wasn't wrong, but she couldn't imagine trusting an entire group of people. It was hard enough for her to be able to trust one or two people at a time, but sixteen other women? How could she place her life in the hands of so many, when at any moment one might betray you for their own selfish gain.

"So what's the right answer then?"

"Only you can decide that. Your choices are your own."

"Who are you?"

"I'm just you, Mimi of the Nowhere. I am just that small, still, inner voice that nags at you. But who I am doesn't matter. I am what you make me. I am your desires and more than anything, you desire to leave behind Nowhere and find a safe and happy home."

Mimi didn't care if she had a safe and happy home, she couldn't remember the last time she lived in one, but she could remember the endless attacks and muggings. She could remember that before she had fully developed her abilities, how vulnerable she was. How could she leave her back exposed to all these women?

"Why did you drink the cup Mimi?"

Mimi thought about it. Why had she shared that cup in the circle? Why had she chosen to gulp down a liquid knowing there were drugs in it? Didn't that make her vulnerable to attack? Wasn't she completely at their mercy?

"You want to trust. You want to love. You want a home. That is why you are here. You want all these things, but you must learn to embrace them. You must learn to unlearn all you have learned in the past. The past is not the present, and if you want it to be, the present is not the future. You decide. You choose. You take your steps forward or back. But ask yourself one question with every step, what will bring you joy and peace?"

And then the woman was gone. The room returned to normal, and she found herself surrounded on all sides by women who were caring for her unconscious form.

"She's awake."

"How...how long was I out?"

"Almost a day."

"Shannon?"

"No word yet."

There was an offer of quarters by Noatla. Several of the sisters had insisted that Mimi not return to her hovel underneath the streets. But it was where Mimi felt at home. Nowhere was all she knew. Why should it be otherwise?

# Chapter 9
# Recycled Runners

TWO DAYS PASSED. DURING the time, Mimi scored some more Likatol to manage the voices, visited the library, and began training with the women of the Order.

The training wasn't terribly difficult. She practiced scanning minds and learned to transmit some of her thoughts to some of the other women. Her thoughts and her focus never strayed far from Shannon. Still, there was no word.

At the end of every day, quarters were offered, sometimes in the library, sometimes with one of her other sisters. She never felt right taking the offer. Her bed still smelled like Shannon and each night returning home, she found herself curling up against the blankets and crying.

On the third night after Shannon's abduction, Mimi lay on her back, turning the events of Shannon's abduction over in her mind. What could she have done differently? What could she have possibly changed? Perhaps if she would have just been with Shannon, then the whole mess could have been avoided?

There was a thick layer of guilt. The weight of it pressed against her chest and made her feel hollowed out. If only she hadn't scared Shannon, hurt her.

She thought of Daniel and the others before her, all the way back to the loss of her mother. The only theme that seemed to reoccur in her life was the loss of loved ones, and in every case, it was her fault. As tears clung to the corner of her eyes, she thought that perhaps she should tell her sisters in the Order that they too would all be doomed if she stuck around. They had been kind to her so far. Mimi was a threat to that kindness.

In that moment, long past the hour of designated dark, in the dim light of the underground where she lived, Mimi resolved to quit the moment Shannon was free. Then, she would ask the sisters to watch over Shannon and disappear into the underground for a while. Her poisonous touch was just too dangerous to continue spreading. Perhaps it was time she seriously considered ending her life.

As it sometimes did, despair took her. It gripped her heart and began to squeeze tight, filling up all the spaces in her heart where love and hope and goodness could live. She sobbed. It was light at first and then violent. She moaned and clenched her jaws and yelled loudly into the night. She cursed the gods and the devils and whatever else was out there. Then she began to look around for something sharp to cut the pain out. A surgical strike. In the corner, she saw the instrument she used to clean the fish. She moved toward it.

A rustling outside. Mimi froze, ears listening.

A crash and a clang of something metal on concrete. Mimi was up in a flash, ready to fight, ready to resist. Her pain augmented her anger, and for one of the first times in her life, Mimi felt ready to draw blood. There was blood in her eyes. She reached for her cutting tool and gripped it firmly.

A hesitant voice. "Hello?" It was soft and feminine. "Mimi, are you here?"

The voice was familiar, but Mimi couldn't place it. Her hackles still raised, her fist white-knuckled around the grip of her tool, she peered her head out of her hovel. She caught a glimpse in the dim designated dark of the underground. She saw only a silhouette. The form of what appeared to be a tiny woman, even shorter than Mimi herself.

It occurred to Mimi that there were probably only a few people in the whole of Manhatsten that could sneak up on her. The thought cooled her.

"Who is it?" Her voice was sharp and low, almost like a growl.

"Leahara. I'm one of your sisters. Do you remember me?"

Mimi thought about it, when they had called names around the circle, she did remember a Leahara. She thought she recalled that she was from the Lowers. She had not trained with her so far.

"Let me see you."

Mimi did not mean see physically, in the last few days, she had learned what seeing meant. It meant to open the mind to your sisters. It was a way of connecting and feeling each other in a deep and intimate way. It was still uncomfortable to Mimi, but she could see that maybe if she spent enough time with the Order, that it might become a good thing.

In the shadows, Leahara nodded, the motion barely visible. There was a burst of thoughts like a burst of color. What was black and white was now vibrant and beautiful.

"You shouldn't sneak up on people like that."

"I'm sorry, it's just...well, an old habit from darker times."

"Darker times?"

Leahara ignored the question. "Can I come in?"

Mimi hesitated for a moment, so far as she could remember she had never brought anyone here before but lovers. Only those she trusted deeply. She felt a bit uneasy but said, "Sure, I guess."

Leahara approached. Her feet barely made a noise.

Mimi joked, "What's your specialty? Invisibility?"

Leahara, her face now visible in the dim light, stood just before the entrance and smiled. "Yes actually. I can make myself very difficult to notice, to some, I may only appear as one of the artificial breezes that the city employs to circulate air and pollen on some occasions."

"Nifty trick."

"I think so."

"Why are you here?"

"Because... well... I believe we have a lot in common and well... it was difficult for me to adjust to being a part of the Order at first."

"How come I haven't seen you in training?"

"Oh... well, I have been taking care of a few things around the city."

Mimi eyed her. Then she stepped back into her hovel and waved her hand gesturing for Leahara to come in. As she passed Mimi, she noticed a woman who was curvy and short. Her hair had streaks of gray in it, and she had a sizable mole on the left cheek. Her eyes were almost a gray color, and her lips were thin.

"I don't employ the alcoves as often as I should," said Leahara.

"Why not?"

"I sometimes struggle with the idea of living a long life."

Mimi was puzzled; she had learned quickly that all the women of the Order, regardless of their status, were sponsored by Noatla, meaning they had the same access she did to the alcoves so that they could continue doing the work for the Order for a good long while.

"Why is that?"

Leahara paused for a moment, then she let Mimi see that she struggled with depression and anxiety. Mimi caught glimpses of a woman huddled in the corner and crying.

"Are all the women of the Order...like us?"

"You mean suffering from some kind of wound or trauma?"

"Yes. I mean, I didn't gain my abilities 'til after something awful happened."

Leahara nodded. "It was the same for me. But, the answer is no. In fact, most of the women of the Order were just born with their abilities. Noatla in particular was born as an Upper and has probably never had a hard day in her life, at least not like we have."

"She seems so strong and wise."

Leahara laughed. "Well, some people get their strength and wisdom from pain and suffering, but for some, it's easy for them, they're born leaders. Noatla has a wonderful heart, but sometimes she doesn't fully understand those of us who have suffered."

Mimi frowned. "Do you sometimes feel like you don't fit in? Like maybe Noatla views you differently?"

"Noatla is Noatla. She treats everyone with respect and loves all of the sisters deeply. It's just that when someone like you or I become part of the Order, she has a hard time understanding things like depression and anxiety. She just can't imagine what it's like. She really does try and shows a great deal of patience, but at the end of the day, her strength comes from a very different source. One very different from yours."

Mimi gestured that she should sit down on the bed. There weren't any chairs, Mimi had put them out the night Shannon had been abducted, along with any other furniture that reminded her of Shannon's absence. Mimi remained standing.

"Mine?"

"Yes, yours. Noatla has told me that you are one of the strongest minds she has ever seen. And that's saying something because Noatla is very powerful."

"Thanks... I guess."

Leahara smiled. "In time, things will make a lot more sense. It takes a while to feel your way around our sisterhood, to find how you fit in."

Mimi squirmed and shifted from foot to foot. "So you said we have something in common?"

Leahara nodded. "I was homeless once. It was only a few weeks before Fatima found me and brought me to the Order, but I've seen what that world is like. I can't imagine being in it for centuries like you were."

"I think I had quite a bit of an advantage over others."

"Obviously, so did I. But that doesn't mean it's not a hard life. Can I ask, why do you keep turning down quarters?"

Mimi squatted down so she was eye level.

Leahara paused for a moment, clearly reading Mimi's thoughts.

"Ah, I see. Trust was hard for me at first too, and no, you aren't betraying Shannon by staying with us."

"Please don't read me like that. I don't like it. Until I can block like the rest of you can, I really would rather you not do that."

Leahara nodded. "Fair enough. I understand that sentiment. I was very uncomfortable with that at first too." She smiled. "You will get used to it."

"Maybe I will, and maybe I won't. I'm not entirely sure if I will stick around." A tinge of anger.

"Well, I hope you do."

"Why?"

"Why what?"

"Why do you care if I stick around."

There was a long pause. In the distance, the sounds of the machinery whirred.

"Because I like you, Mimi. I think you have a good heart."

"You only met me a few days ago and we haven't even spoken. How could you possibly know that?"

"I just do. And I see a woman who has had nothing but a life full of pain and suffering. And, I guess... well, I want you to know that if you stay with us, we can help you. We can keep you safe so you don't have to peer over your shoulder every night. You won't have to go and hack a food dispenser anymore or sneak into an alcove."

Mimi felt a tightness in her chest. She couldn't trace the source but she also couldn't help taking it out on this woman either. "Sounds like one of those Uppers clubs you hear rumors about. The ones where they bring up people from the lowers, fuck them, and then send them off to the Runnercore afterward."

Leahara was visibly hurt. She looked down at the floor and crossed her arms.

"No... it's..."

"Why are you really down here? Did Noatla send you or something? Are we required to live in assigned quarters or something?"

"No... I..."

There was a pause and then the rasping shutter of Leahara's throat as she began to sob.

Mimi's mouth opened and shut. Why was she so mean to this woman? What had she done to her? But Mimi knew, this woman had come to her space, without permission, but that was only part of it. Mimi was angry at herself for Shannon and that guilt would throb in her chest until Shannon was free.

Mimi said, "I'm sorry. I... I'm not very good with strangers."

"I know. It's just... well... I once had a daughter that looked very much like you. She was bright and beautiful and so full of joy and love."

Mimi shifted in her crouch. She bit her lip. "She's a Runner now?"

Leahara shook her head. "Worse."

A chill crept over Mimi. "Re...Recycled?" She didn't even like to say the word out loud. There was horror in it.

Leahara burst into tears. Mimi stood and walked over and sat down next to her. The woman's entire body convulsed with sobs and a run of snot cascaded down her nose. Mimi pulled her in close, feeling her warmth. There was comfort there for both of them. Leahara wiped her nose on her sleeve and then put her head on Mimi's shoulder.

"When?"

Leahara swallowed. "Only a few months ago."

The wound was still fresh. Mimi realized why this woman was down here. She wasn't trying to comfort her, she was looking for comfort.

"Why haven't you told the other sisters?"

"I can't."

"Why not?"

"I don't know. It's just... I don't think they would understand?"

"Why do you think that I would understand?"

Leahara lifted her head and looked into Mimi's eyes. "Because someone you love was just taken by the SOs. Because you've lived down here for a reason, at some point everything must have been taken from you." She buried her head back in Mimi's chest, nuzzling her and soaking Mimi's shirt with tears.

Mimi thought for a moment. She hesitated, but decided that maybe this woman would understand. "The last man I loved... he was before Shannon, they recycled him."

Leahara looked up again. "What happened?"

"It's a long story."

"Tell me." It was not a question. It was a demand.

Mimi frowned. "You first."

Leahara lifted her head and eyed Mimi for a moment and then opened her mouth to speak. She coughed a little and cleared her throat and then looked toward Mimi's door for a moment. "She was only twenty-nine."

Leahara's eyes were glassy and the streaks of tears left a silver sheen down her face. "It wasn't even really her fault. She was just out one night with friends celebrating her birthday. She had started a job working in the sanitation department. It was a stable job. You know how hard it is to find a stable job in this city, right?"

Mimi nodded. She had tried for more than a century to live as a Lower, but was never able to find a steady or stable job for more than a few years and so eventually gave up. It was easier to live in her hovel than it was to keep an apartment.

"She was grateful. You know, some people who work hard in the sanitation department and pick up extra shifts can sometimes move up into the Lower-Mids, only the 10th - 12th levels in the buildings, but it extends their life for a few more centuries and gives them a chance to have more than one child and it's much more comfortable."

Mimi nodded. Leahara put her head in her hands again and started to sob.

Through her tears she continued, occasionally pausing to catch her breath. "I thought she was safe. Lucy wasn't the prettiest of girls. You know how dangerous it is to be pretty in the Lowers. But still, somehow she caught the eye of an SO. Apparently, from what I heard later, he had been following her around for weeks, making propositions. He even cornered her one night and forced her to kiss him. She got away, thank god, but after that first encounter she never walked alone again."

"The night of her birthday she was with four friends. I don't know what happened, but somehow she got separated. Maybe the SO figured out a way to separate her from her group, or maybe she was intoxicated and wandered off without thinking. In either case, she ended up alone and of course, who should appear?"

Mimi shivered. She had narrowly escaped similar encounters several times. If she had not been able to skim minds, she might have ended up on the wrong side of that situation. Being a woman on the streets was a dangerous game, much worse for the homeless because you had to worry about every male predator out there and without shelter, there was almost no escape from the endless moments of watching your back. Without Mimi's hovel and knowledge, she didn't know how she would have survived so long. Somehow Shannon had avoided that fate. Shannon knew of the dangers, but she had managed to avoid almost all of them and without any special abilities.

"Lucy told me before they took her to the Runner Docks that he tried to get her to come home with him. But see, even though Lucy knew what the consequences would be, she started carrying a taser. Lord knows where she got it. It's a black-market item. But when the Security Officer wouldn't leave her alone... she pulled it out. She said she gave him a warning, and she told this to the judge. I watched her testimony.

"Apparently this man had a rare heart condition. The alcoves kept him from ever having to worry about any serious medical issues of course, but he was susceptible to heart attacks. When he grabbed at Lucy, she used the taser on him. He had a heart attack, and because it's been centuries since anyone has had to treat one no one knew what to do. He died before they could get him to an alcove. He was dead just a little too long for the alcove to revive him."

"But... it was an accident, wasn't it?" said Mimi.

"The Supreme Justices didn't seem to care about that. They said that Lucy had an illegal weapon that she must have obtained through illegal means. Then she used that weapon and took a life. You know how high of a crime it is to take human life in this city. It might seem like the two million or so we have here are a lot, that it's crowded, but these cities are the only lifeboats left to us. So, they said murder, even an accident, is punishable by exile. And you know what exile means."

"The Runnercore." Mimi's voice was just above a whisper. "But how did she end up recycled?"

Leahara shook her head through more tears. "Serah told me."

"I thought you said none of the other sisters knew?"

"Serah does, and she promised to keep it secret if that's what I wanted. No one but her knew about Lucy's conviction."

Mimi put a pin in that for a moment. She had to know why she wanted to keep this secret. Maybe there was something about the Order that Leahara didn't trust? First, though, she wanted to know how Lucy became recycled. "So...how did it happen, then?"

"Did you know that when someone becomes a part of the Runnercore, they inject a bunch of chemicals in their body?"

Mimi nodded. She knew that they augmented strength to deal with the massive walking armor the Runners wore, and she had once skimmed that the chemicals also helped with keeping them in semi-stasis in the alcoves until they unboxed Runners for duty, but she wasn't sure how it worked.

"Well," said Leahara, "in rare cases, some people are allergic to the chemicals. Their body can't tolerate them. Serah told me it's less than one percent, but she has seen it happen before. She..."

Leahara wept. Her whole body shook. She started to moan like an animal injured and dying in the wilderness alone. Mimi gripped on to her tight. She focused her mind in the way she had been learning and tried to project happy thoughts of peace, love, and joy into Leahara.

It seemed to work a little. Leahara reached up and grabbed one of Mimi's hands and squeezed it.

"Thank you, Mimi. This is why I came to you."

Mimi didn't entirely understand what Leahara meant, but it seemed that there was no time for asking.

"She died. On the table. Then they took her to that facility underground."

Mimi had stood outside the doors. There was no apparent way in. When she had lost Daniel, she had gone to the giant doors and looked for one. She had wanted to stop his conversion.

Mimi asked, "Does Serah know... what they do in that place?"

Leahara shook her head. "No, she said she doesn't think anyone does. She said she doesn't even think that any humans work there. The rumors are, the recycled themselves do the processing. That the city AI directs them, but Serah said she has worked for a long time with the AI now, and she doesn't see how the AI is capable of that. It isn't fully aware, but she said that she doesn't think the AI can do harm, something about three laws or something."

Mimi said, "Maybe the AI doesn't think it's doing any harm because the people it converts to recycled are already dead?"

Leahara's face was pale. "Maybe."

"Does Serah know why they recycle them? Why they bring them back to life?"

Again, Leahara shook her head. "Serah says that in this city nothing should be wasted, at least that's the idea. When the city started running the biorecyclers and breaking down organic components into ingredients for the algae pools, everyone decided immediately that human corpses wouldn't be a part of that process. No one, Lowers, Mids, or Uppers, could tolerate the idea that they might be eating human remains, even though the biorecycler breaks all organics down into subatomic material and reassembles it again. Still, the idea was intolerable."

Mimi said, "So Serah says the recycled were a way of making sure that the parts still got used even though they were dead?"

Leahara nodded.

Mimi asked, "But what if the body is damaged beyond repair? Like, all of the recycled have a full body and a head, I've never seen one that was... incomplete."

"I don't know, Mimi. All I know is, she is down there now."

"Did you... did you see her after?"

Leahara leaked fresh tears and nodded her head.

"But how?"

Leahara wiped her nose on her sleeve. "I begged Serah. She didn't want me to see. She said that no good would come of it, but I begged her until she relented. Now, I wish I hadn't."

Mimi had never seen Daniel's face in person, but she would never be able to forget what she saw just before Shannon's abduction, that vision or whatever it was, was burned into her memory. She had seen other recycled Runners before, and she knew how terrifying they looked.

"It was horrible, Mimi. Her face was blank and pale white with these strange blue lines all over it. I think they were her veins but there were so many. And her eyes..."

Mimi tried to keep the image of those white on white on white orbs out of her head, but she couldn't. It was as if someone had scooped out the eyes and replaced it with a pure white marble.

"But still. I was her mother. And despite it all, I ran for her. I ran to hold her in my arms, even though she was in one of those giant metallic suits. Serah tried to stop me but she couldn't. I wrapped my arms around her as best I could. I tried to feel her warmth, but her face was far too high up because she was in one of the suits. More than anything, I wanted to kiss her forehead, but do you know what happened?"

Mimi shook her head.

"Nothing. Nothing happened. She acted as if she was a lifeless doll, some kind of manikin. I screamed at her to respond, to let me know she was alive but... Lucy wasn't in there anymore."

Leahara collapsed completely into Mimi's arms. She gave up all her strength and let it run out of her as if it was some kind of liquid that filled the body and ran down into the ground.

Mimi didn't want to ask. But she had to. "Leahara." She stroked her hair gently, the way that she remembered her mother used to do to her when she was upset.

Leahara didn't respond.

"Leahara, why can't you tell the other sisters?"

More silence. Echoing moans. Sniffling.

Mimi didn't think an answer would come. Then it did.

"What would the other sisters think of me? How could I let that happen to my child? I have this talent, this gift, and I was unable to use it to stop my own daughter from being taken from me. How could they accept me into their ranks if they knew I was such a failure? They would cast me out if they knew. It's the only home I have left, Mimi."

Mimi understood. Then she understood something else. Mimi thought of what her mother would have said to her.

"Leahara, do you really believe that your sisters are your family?"

She nodded.

"Then you have to trust them. You have to know they will understand. You have to know that they will want to help you through this, don't you?"

Mimi was confused by the words that were coming out of her mouth for a moment; they had been so automatic. Buried treasure. Her mother had raised her as well as she could. Her mother had always been there for her, even if it was only until that terrible night. Yes, her mother might have been a drug addict at the end, but never had her mother failed to comfort her when she was sad or lonely. Never had her mother neglected her in any way and perhaps her mother had only turned to drugs to shoulder the burden that each man brought with him into her bed. For the first time in her life, Mimi thought she might understand all those things that her mother had said about family. It was like a faint outline of knowing, one that could, over time, be filled in.

"Family is there for each other Leahara, as best as they can be. Sometimes it's the little things. Sometimes they are distanced because they have to be. Sometimes they do things that we don't understand. And sometimes the best families are the ones that we make in life, not the ones we are born with. Trust them Leahara, tell them what happened. I can comfort you a little, but... I'm not so good at this. I... I haven't had a family in a very long time."

Leahara looked up. "You're right. Tomorrow will you come with me? Will you help me tell them?"

"Yes."

"Can I... Can I stay here with you tonight?"

"Yes."

Mimi laid her sister down on the bed gently and then laid down next to her. She wrapped her arms around her and before long, they slept.

# Chapter 10
# News

MOST OF THE SISTERS gathered in a group around Leahara as she told her story. Noatla and Serah were absent on some errand, but the others listened eagerly.

After, tears and embraces were traded. Healing, like water on a smoldering fire. Even Mimi felt a sense of relief. She suspected that each sister was soothing the other in turn, calming one another's emotions.

Leahara said, "Mimi, will you share your story of how your lover became recycled?"

Mimi frowned. She hadn't been expecting this. She had thought she had gotten away with not telling Leahara the whole story, but she had been wrong. The other sisters waited patiently for her to begin.

"I... in truth, I haven't even been able to speak of it to Shannon. I don't know if I can tell it to all of you."

Leahara said, "You're in a safe space, Mimi." She grabbed Mimi's hand.

Mimi cleared her mind to transmit; rarely now was she using her mouth to communicate with her sisters. Then, the door to the library archive burst open and in walked Noatla and Serah. All was forgotten.

"Is Mimi here?" Noatla said, scanning the room.

Mimi's heart sank. Noatla wasn't blocking her. She let Mimi see everything. Serah couldn't even look her in the face.

"Shannon's already been sentenced?"

Noatla nodded.

# Chapter 11
# New Beginnings

FOR SHANNON, THE PASSAGE of time had elongated, days reached crooked fingers into the centuries and grasped tightly as she lay on her back and stared at the ceiling.

After the arrest she had been taken to central security, the building that had stood the highest in all of the city of Manhatsten. She had no idea what floor they had taken her to, but when she exited the lift, she swore it looked like the underground that she and Mimi had explored. There were only a handful of cells, but all were occupied, save two. One for Andrew and one for herself.

Andrew had been processed quickly. He had disappeared the morning after they had been arrested and had not returned. Shannon assumed that had meant one of two things. Either he was free, or he was now a Runner. She assumed that the second was far more likely, from what she had heard, once someone was arrested they almost always became a Runner.

There were low mutterings from the other prisoners but she couldn't make them out. Occasionally she would hear someone weeping. The floor was cold and there was no way to hide when she needed to use the bathroom. She held it for as long as she could and then tried to wait 'til none of the guards were around. None of them peeked in at her, but she still felt exposed.

The food came twice a day. The funny thing was, she was eating better and was probably safer then she had ever been on the street, except when she was with Mimi.

Why had Andrew been processed so quickly, but she so slowly? Was that a good sign? She couldn't see how it would be considered a bad sign. If they were taking longer, did that mean they were unsure of what to do with her?

She marked the time by the change in the guards' shifts. Her second and third day of captivity she spent most of her time imagining the moment when Mimi would sneak in to free her. Together, they would escape into the underground world that Mimi lived and they would live down there for the rest of their lives, never to surface again.

Maybe Shannon could even use the alcove that Mimi was using and maybe they would be happy, just the two of them, for centuries. Shannon thought she would like that, that it would be a wonderful way to spend the rest of her days. After all, the last few weeks with Mimi had been the best of her life, despite Mimi accidentally hurting her.

She decided that it had been an accident and that she forgave Mimi. It would be the first thing she said to her when she saw her. Shannon was certain that Mimi would never do something like that. She had one of the kindest hearts she had ever met, even if she always acted tough and empathetic.

EARLY ON HER FOURTH day of captivity, Shannon was summoned to trial.

She entered the courtroom. It almost looked like an office. Seven men and women sat in chairs, deliberating. One of them, the one in the center who didn't look a day over thirty-five but sat in the rigid posture of someone much older, was reviewing something on a data tablet.

His voice was gruff and deep. "Shannon, you have been charged with aggravated assault on a security officer and in trafficking in illicit substances. How do you plead?"

Shannon looked around the room. "I... I don't understand." She looked at her feet.

One of the women on the end gave a heavy sigh. "He is asking if you admit to dealing drugs and assaulting a security officer."

"Oh. Um, no, I... um... of course I didn't do those things." Tears began to pour down her cheeks. It was involuntary. "Please your honors, I've never hurt anyone. Please don't make me a Runner."

One of the judges reclined in their chair. The others sat rigid. The one who reclined said, "Tell us your story. Please note that we will know if you are lying."

So Shannon did. She did her best to leave Mimi out of the story, which made it difficult to tell. She was afraid that if she mentioned Mimi, they would go after her too. After all, how could she possibly explain that Mimi could read minds and needed Likatol to find a sense of peace from the voices of the city? She would sound crazy, and from what she understood, crazy people became Runners too.

"That's quite a story. So you are telling us, that this man Andrew wanted to kidnap you because he believed he could get some leverage over another dealer? Why would he believe that?"

"Because the other dealer had a thing for me. I never dated him or anything, but he was always doing favors for me, and he clearly liked me. I think Andrew thought that we were a couple and that he could blackmail this man into working with him."

That seemed to pause the judges for a moment. They leaned in and consulted one another. Mimi would have been proud. The story seemed to make some sense, at least. She was getting better at lying. Mimi was a good teacher.

"And what of the Security Officer, you said that he was a part of this too?"

Shannon nodded. She had the slightest sense of hope. They seemed to be discussing at length now. There was some kind of debate over at last part of her story. If there were some sort of disagreement, maybe that would mean that at least some of them believed her.

The judge in the center spoke up as they group split back apart. "We will have to deliberate on this for a while. Please follow the Security Officer back to your cell and await our decision."

THE DOOR TO HER CELL closed behind her with a hard click. She sat back on her bed. One way or another, her life on the streets was over. If she was set free, she would never come to the surface again, at least not without Mimi and never for long. If she became a Runner, that was a different set of problems.

She had only been on the streets for a handful of years, driven there by her father. He was a drunk, and Shannon had watched her mother put up with it for years. Some nights, Shannon would wake to the sounds of angry yells and loud thuds. In the morning, her mother would have fresh bruises on her face, reddened wrists, and a quiet demeanor.

One night, when she was nineteen, her father came into her room drunk and began shouting at her over a water ration. She shouted back. He had gotten drunk and left the shower running and she had tried to point that out to him. Soon enraged, he hit her. She left. She never went back. Her mother might be willing to put up with his shit, but she had not been. She wondered how they were doing now, if her father still had a job repairing alcoves, or if he had been fired again. Was her mother still with him? If she were set free, maybe she would check up on them.

SHE DIDN'T WAIT LONG, she had no idea how much time had passed, but she felt certain it had been at least a few hours. When the door opened, a single guard stepped in. Her face betrayed nothing. But then, how or why would she know what the Supreme Justices had decided? The woman was probably in the dark as much as Shannon was.

Shannon noticed her flaming red hair pulled back into a pony-tail. It looked unnatural that way, like the hair was normally free, but stuck confined.

They walked down several corridors and finally arrived at the long hall. Before the woman ushered her in through the door, she said. "Good luck." This puzzled Shannon, why would she care what happened to her?

She stepped in through the door, and it closed behind her. She walked up to where she had stood earlier and waited. All seven justices stared at her.

"Shannon Ulstis?"

Shannon said, "Yes, your honors?"

"Please approach us."

Shannon did as she was told and moved closer. Now only two meters from the judges, she stopped and waited. She felt the hairs on the back of her neck raise. It was an odd feeling, having your entire life decided by a few people who you've never met before.

She glanced back and saw two armed SOs, but neither were paying much attention. One almost appeared to be dozing.

Could she escape? If she could push through those men and out of central security, maybe she stood a chance. She didn't know the city as well as Mimi, but she was certain she could find some sort of entrance to the underground nearby, and once down there she could hide for a while until she figured out how to get back to Mimi.

But then, what if they said she was free to go? Would she be sentenced to the Runnercore for trying to run away? Maybe the judges would change their mind if they saw her trying to run.

She turned back to the judges.

"Shannon Ulstis, we have considered your case carefully. The testimony of one Andrew Melborne, and one Jerry McKinley were considered in our decision."

There was something in the man's voice that made Shannon certain of what was coming. She felt the urge to run rise. Her feet twitched, hungry for quick motion.

The judge was droning on about how they had come to their decision, about whose testimony had more weight and about some surveillance footage they had obtained for the trial.

Shannon heard none of this and when the judge said, "We find you not guilty on the charge of aggravated assault. However, we find you guilty of trafficking illegal substances," Shannon had already submitted to her desire.

It was like watching someone from the outside. Things moved in slow motion as she ran through the benches and leaped over a barrier toward the door, and the SOs came to life. The shorter one, who had been dozing, was looking around confused. She easily dodged both the guards and ran through the door. But as she got just outside and into the hall, she slammed into something large and hard.

It was Jerry, the man who had tried to double cross Andrew and sell her to the Uppers.

"Well, well, well. Look who's run into me all over again."

His smile made her stomach cramp as he reached down and grabbed her. He picked up her body and threw it back into the courtroom. She crashed to the floor, slamming her head against one of the benches.

Yelling into the room, but not quite entering it, Jerry said, "So you just gonna let this one escape or what?"

All went black.

SHANNON WOKE ON A SMALL moving platform in the middle of a large open area. She glanced around, looking at the endless open space of concrete. Above, a high ceiling was occasionally punctuated with a number of mechanical arms, but mostly the ceiling was smooth and gray.

She turned her head to the side and saw that there were many raised platforms with short steps leading to the top directly below the mechanical arms. In the distant corners of the enormous space, there were small stand-alone buildings. Each was one story high. A small square in the massive open space.

Two men were escorting her. Both were in large metal suits.

"Where... where am I?" her voice shook.

Neither stopped. Neither turned. Neither answered.

She raised her voice. "Hey. Where am I?"

Still no response.

Her heart started to pound in her ears. An icy hand wrapped around her throat and it became harder to breathe

She yelled this time. "Where am I?"

Silence, a violent silence.

She tried to move and realized that she was strapped down. There was no escape, no movement.

The two forms marched her forward through the open area.

She screamed. All the pain and rage and sorrow in her released and she struggled to gain her freedom. But a part of her knew the truth. That her freedom had vanished, that the last choices she would ever have to make had been in the few moments that her and Mimi had spent together. Now her choices would be dictated by the city for the rest of her life, however long or short that life was.

Her voice grew hoarse, and when, after several moments of screaming, there was no wind left in her, she sobbed silently. Her escorts betrayed no interest.

Finally, they were moving through a set of large metal doors. Just after entering, her escorts stopped. The stretcher hovered forward between the metal encased men. As it did, she finally had a look at their faces. Her blood froze. Her breath escaped, terrified to come back.

Their faces were deathly pale. Thin blue lines traced all the major muscles in their faces. Their eyes were the worst, naked white with no pupils. As she passed between them, they both tilted their heads towards her. With all white eyes, it was impossible to tell where they were looking, but she knew, beyond all possible doubt that they were staring right at her, that somehow, they were seeing her.

Mimi had been right. There were things in this city worse than being a runner. She had never discovered her meaning, but now she knew firsthand the awful truth. She wondered if this was what happened when a Runner died. If so, then even in death there was no peace. She must stay alive as long as possible.

She wept as she floated on through another set of doors. She heard them shut behind her as the table to which she was strapped settled. She lifted upward. The table swung so that her feet were toward the ground and her head raised up as if she was standing.

A person in a mask appeared. All clad in black save for one white mask. She could see only his brown eyes. He regarded her only for a moment and then examined a set of tools that lay just to the right of her in a tray. Sharp objects for cutting. He selected one.

"Where am I?" said Shannon.

Silence, except for the thin sound of cloth on skin. For Shannon, that sound was abrasive. When the person picked up one of the metal instruments, the one that looked like a mix between a saw and a knife, every clink of the metal felt so loud that she thought her ears would bleed. Her heartbeat started a rhythmic thumping as he approached, tool in hand.

"Oh dear gods, what are you doing? Please."

The person hesitated and stared at her for a moment. Shannon looked long and hard into those eyes, and for that moment she saw something human. Whoever it was, it wasn't like the things that had escorted her into the room.

Through veils of tears and blurred vision, she begged. "Please talk to me, please just tell me what you are doing. Are you... turning me... into one of those things?"

The person paused. A deer in the headlights. They lowered the tool for a moment. Then, with great hesitation, they reached up and drew down the mask.

It was a woman. Her face was hard and her jaw matched. Her brown eyes regarded her harshly.

She said, "I know not what you did to be here, but no, I am not Recycling you. I don't think they would let a human do that. This is the first step to becoming a Runner. I won't lie to you, what is about to happen to you is going to hurt. In fact, depending on your constitution, it may hurt tremendously."

Shannon quivered. Her tears did not hesitate.

"Please don't cry like that. I don't want to do this to you any more than you want to have it done." The woman's voice wavered.

"Please. Just let me go. I'll disappear."

The woman grinned. "Disappear? To where? Where in this city could you possibly vanish to where you wouldn't be found?"

Shannon almost said something about the underground area, almost told this woman of Mimi in her desperation. If she was just able to get to Mimi, she knew that Mimi could hide her, keep her safe. Mimi would know when someone was coming, would know exactly how to protect Shannon.

"We must all do our part if we want to city to survive," said the woman. "Everyone must have a function; how else can humanity continue? Even the dead serve a purpose here, as you just saw. Even the dead are recycled when they can be."

"Please, you don't understand, I do have a place to go, a place to hide."

The woman shook her head, "You are not the first to claim this and once long ago, I probably would have believed you. Perhaps a century ago I would have let you escape. But look."

The table swiveled toward the door. On either side of the door was viewing glass, and Shannon could see both creatures standing and staring from outside. A mindful horror.

"You see, long ago, I did let someone escape. In fact, I was almost made a Runner myself, but instead, they returned me to work. They knew that I let a woman go because I was weak, that the best way to punish me was to grant me the status of an Upper and force me, year after year, century after century, to be one of the ones who had to perform the surgeries on the new Runners."

The chair rotated back.

The woman shook her head, and a single tear descended the landscape of her cheek. She did not wipe it away. "I weep for you. I weep for them all. But mostly, I weep for them." She gestured towards the Recycled. "But weeping does not change my fate. So please, do not make this harder on me. Please do not fight me, for I too am here being punished. You, like me, are now just a cog in the wheel, a body that keeps the machine running, the city walking, a kind of perpetual cycle. We cannot stop it. We must do our part."

She reached up and covered her face again. "For what it's worth, I'm sorry."

The woman went behind her. Shannon tingled. She had no idea what was coming, but as a restraint leaped up over her forehead and pulled tight, she expected the worst.

A voice came from behind her. "I will give you something for the pain. It is not something I always do. Some of the people who come through here deserve every bit of pain they get. Some of those who become Runners are rapists and monsters. But I suspect that you are not one of these. I suspect that you are one of the innocent ones. Maybe you were caught in the games of one of the politicians, I don't know. There is little I can offer you but this."

Shannon felt a sharp poking sensation in the back of her neck and was suddenly aware of the large hole in the table at that exact spot. It was ice and fire and the burning spread quickly through her body. She yelled out in pain, but just as she started to yell, the burning became warmth. She felt an overwhelming urge to urinate but just as she thought her bladder would burst, or her bowels would let go, the warmth became a void. Her entire body went numb.

Shannon wanted to say something, that for this at least she was grateful, but even her tongue was incapable of response. Her eyelids felt like great metal doors as they continued to blink, but the effort to move them was monumental. She wasn't sleepy, on the contrary, she was wide awake and fully aware, it was just that her body no longer felt there, only her mind seemed to be present.

The woman continued, "Now I am going to install your obedience chip. This will ensure your cooperation as a Runner. All Runners possess them, and if you disobey, you will receive a painful shock up and down your spine. This will most likely not kill you, but it will be incredibly painful. If, however, you are perceived as a threat, the chip can be used to end your life. Understand that if your life ends in this way, you will be recycled as those two who escorted you were."

Shannon wanted to ask if those men were still conscious, if they were still alive, if they had anything left of themselves, but her tongue simply wouldn't work.

"You will now feel a strong pressure."

She did, it was like a hand was squeezing the back of her neck hard, but there was no pain, only pressure. There was a drilling noise. There was the smell of flesh and blood, tangy and pungent like uncooked meat.

"Are you still with me?" the woman asked. "Ah forgive me, I forgot, the numbing agent sometimes takes the speech, I use it so rarely." She walked around front.

"Blink if you are with me."

Shannon did.

"Your chip is installed, and I have placed a regeneration patch on the wound. Within a few hours, it will be completely healed. Now, we must augment your muscles."

The table tilted backward and Shannon found herself lying flat and staring at the ceiling.

"Unfortunately, this process will cause rather violent muscle spasms. There is little I can do for this part of the process; despite the numbing agent, it will still be somewhat painful."

Shannon blinked.

The woman went on, and Shannon thought that perhaps explaining it eased the woman's burden.

"The pain is from the nanites. The nanites will work their way into all the muscles in your body and release a series of growth hormones. This will cause your muscles to double or triple in strength based on your genetic potential. It will allow you to pilot the EnViro suits. Without the added strength, you would not be able to do so for long. The nanites will also grant you much greater endurance when you are out in the barrens, what we call the world outside the city. I will begin now. I will not blame you if you scream. Do whatever it is you need to do. This will pass, and you will be stronger for it, but it will not be pleasant."

The band that held Shannon's forehead released and she was free to move her head around again and watch the woman work.

The woman brought over a long tube. At the tip was a sharp metal needle. She plunged it into Shannon's left bicep. Then she brought another tube and plunged it into her left thigh. The woman worked for a few more moments, plugging these tubes into various points in Shannon's body.

A loud buzzing noise began. Shannon had heard something like it once before, a beehive in Central Park. Her father had told her as a child that the bees used to be living creatures, but now they were just tiny robots. Her father had said that the creatures still made the same noises as the machines.

Then the pain came, white-hot and searing. Her body was electric fire. It felt as if someone was holding her entire body in an oven and she was cooking. She almost swore she could smell her own flesh burning. The pain increased steadily. Shannon began to scream.

In the breaks between screams, the sliver of seconds in that space, she looked over in the corner where the woman sat. Her mask was off, her face was buried, and tears leaked between her knuckles.

Shannon decided to stop screaming. She let the pain take her. In a river, drowning. She retreated into her mind.

# Chapter 12
# The Red Veil

THE ANGER CAME IN WAVES. She was a boat in a storm, solitary and surrounded by a savage sadness.

Mimi sat in the circle of her new sisters and stewed.

Serah said, "The chip's been installed already. I'm not sure there's much we can do."

Leahara said, "There must be something."

Serah shook her head. "The problem is the chip. The chip can track her anywhere in the city. If I had been able to get to her before the chip was installed, we could have snuck her out and hidden her. But for some reason, she was processed immediately. That never happens."

Noatla looked at Serah. "What do you mean, that never happens?"

"Well, usually the sentence is given, and it's at least two weeks before the new Runner is processed. The only exception I can think of is if we are in dire need of Runners, or if there is a pending battle, but that's definitely not an issue right now." Serah looked at Mimi. "Really, the whole thing is strange."

Mimi asked, "What do you mean?"

"Well, I was there. The justices deliberated. The initial vote was 6 to 3 in favor of letting her go free. They seemed to agree that she was just some poor young girl caught up in a bad situation she didn't understand. I mean, the Supreme Justices aren't total monsters, although when it comes to the Uppers, well..."

Mimi asked. She was crouched now and leaning forward. "So, what happened?"

"Well, they usually take a first vote to see where everyone sits and then each of the justices speaks their peace. When they're finished, they take a final vote. When they got to Allistair, the chief justice, who had initially voted to clear her... I don't know... it was strange."

Noatla cocked her head. "Go on."

"Look, I don't remember all of what he said, but some of it didn't make a damn bit of sense. It was something about the red curtains or drapes or something."

"A red veil?" Her voice emphasized the question. Noatla's eyes were wide. Her entire demeanor changed.

"Yes, a red veil, but I don't remember much else, and it's almost like... well like I saw something red."

Mimi stood up. "I've seen red lately too."

Noatla said, "Where, Mimi? Tell us everything. Don't skip anything."

Mimi related the events when she and Shannon were nearly caught by the two sanitation workers. She told them how their thoughts just disappeared, how one of the workers had insisted that she had heard something, while the other almost seemed afraid of going their direction.

"The one afraid of going your direction, that was me," said Noatla. "I couldn't understand why the woman in the pair was so insistent. But you are sure you saw red?"

Mimi nodded. "I won't forget it. It was like something red veiled my vision." She cast her eyes downward. "This wasn't the only time."

Mimi told them about the night when she had scared Shannon and made her head hurt and the few other moments when she seemed almost on the verge of losing control of her emotions. Then, she spoke of her experience during her initiation and how the red shadow had passed her by.

Noatla looked almost pale. All softness had left her face, only strong ridges remained. "Mimi, why didn't you share any of this with us before?"

Mimi thought about it. It was a good question. "Maybe because I didn't think it related in any way to what happened to Shannon. My mind's been so focused on her, I hardly think of anything else."

Noatla seemed to accept this answer. In a low voice, barely above a whisper, she said, "It just can't be."

Fatima said, "She's dead, Noatla." Sisters Kayla and Yoshi echoed the sentiment.

"We never did find the body, though," she said.

Fatima said, "No but that was two centuries ago and before the destruction of the city of Mex. Mex was where she was living, and you know it. Her madness destroyed that city."

Mimi said, "Who are you talking about?"

Noatla looked puzzled for a moment, and then her face cleared. "It's nothing, Mimi. It's something to worry about another day. But Serah, what happened after the judge spoke those words?"

"Two of them changed their votes, and she was convicted 5 to 4 and put in processing immediately, which as I said, never happens unless it's an emergency."

"Do you think it was her, Noatla?" Leahara said.

Noatla looked thoughtful for a moment "It seems very unlikely. And anyway, she wasn't the only one to use the Red Veil. She wasn't the only rogue sister out there. Most cities have had a rogue sister in their order. It could be another. It could even be someone untrained we don't know about. It can't possibly be her, Fatima is right."

Mimi didn't like this. Rogue sisters? Red Veils? She spoke up. "What the hell does all that mean?"

Noatla said, "For now Mimi, let me just say that there are other women out there with our abilities. Some of them are trained and accept the Order, some of them choose to be on their own. Once in a while, a sister will leave the Order and go rogue. Usually, this means she chooses to use her abilities for selfish gain and breaks our taboos."

"The red veil?"

"It's when someone tries to force another human being into doing something. We aren't sure exactly why you see red, but if enough force is used, the brain begins to hemorrhage. We think that the red tinge in vision comes from the mind trying to interpret that damage, but we aren't sure."

Mimi considered for a moment. "You said it was dangerous, though."

Noatla seemed to hesitate for a moment. "Yes, it is." Noatla stood and paced around the room. All eyes were on her. "Mimi, this isn't something we normally tell new sisters. Normally we want you to understand your own abilities for a while before we impart this information. But if something is going on, you need to know this."

Mimi shifted back to a sitting position. Her throat felt dry. Most of her moisture had departed through her tear ducts.

"It is possible to use the red veil without too much damage to yourself or others."

Mimi waited. Noatla seemed to be choosing her words carefully. The surface of her mind shifted back and forth between blank canvas and a fully flushed-out landscape of knowledge.

"Once in a while, a woman joins the Order whose specialty is the red veil, who can push others into doing something they wouldn't normally do. It is much more than the usual manipulation of emotions. It is control."

"A long time ago, when the cities were first excavated from their bedrock, and the architects began the migration, there was a kind of accident. A woman with extraordinary abilities was born in an alcove. We don't fully understand what happened. All we know is what this woman told us."

"What was her name?"

Noatla hesitated for a few moments. "We don't really like to talk about her, you see. She was the antithesis of everything we stand for. Her name was..." Noatla swallowed. Several of the sisters in the room shifted uncomfortably, but Mimi noticed that not all of them did. She had learned quickly that a few of them, like Serah, were much newer to the Order. Only a handful of the women had been around for centuries.

"Her name was Miranda. She told us that she was born in an alcove when the city took its first steps. She said that she was born because her mother was killed in the alcove, crushed by a piece of rubble. That she was stuck inside of it, which somehow still functioned despite the damage, for almost a decade."

Fatima interrupted. "She was mad. We don't know if she was telling the truth or not. She claimed that all of her mother's memories were implanted into her, that somehow the alcove interpreted her mother's DNA and hers as one entity and so it remade her, not as two people but as one. This is her claim, but she was utterly mad."

Mimi said, "Then why did you welcome her into the Order?"

Noatla replied, "We didn't know she was mad, at first. She hid it well."

Kayla said, "Or maybe she wasn't mad then. Maybe she was just a bit disturbed and, when she realized what her specialty was, that she could force people into doing things they didn't want to do, she became hungry for power, and maybe that drove her mad."

Noatla said, "She went rogue. She attacked us, and when she couldn't fight all of us together, she fled to Mex. We didn't know where she went at first and we still don't know how she managed to get to another city but one day four-and-a-half centuries ago, when Manhatsten and Mex were in trade negotiations, the Order of the Eye from Mex attacked us and with it, their Runners attacked ours. The only thing that saved us was that one of our Runners managed to break through the battle and disable Mex's EnViro shield. Their entire city had to shut down while Mex reset it and Manhatsten was able to flee."

Mimi had remembered that battle. It was the one when she had discovered the power of Benadextrin.

Mimi asked, "How in the world did a Runner disable the shields?"

Noatla smiled. "Well, this is no ordinary Runner, I am sure you have heard of him."

The only Runner Mimi had ever heard of was the one that everyone had heard of, that films on the vid screen had been made about, Runner 17.

Noatla nodded. "Yes, him. Somehow, he managed to sneak past everyone and disable the shield. No one, at least no one I have discussed this with, quite understands how. It would require all kinds of clearance codes that Runner 17 couldn't possibly have, that no one in our city could possibly have. But he did it, and because of him, Miranda failed."

"Then, almost two centuries later, Mex was destroyed. No one knows why, but we suspect that Miranda had something to do with it. No one without an EnViro suit can survive for more than a few hours outside of a city, and there were no cities within a few hundred kilometers of Mex when the city collapsed. Later there were many cities, for when a city falls, the others will turn up to scavenge its resources, but it was weeks before another city came across Mex."

Mimi said, "So this red veil was her specialty?"

"Yes, but we've had other sisters in the past who were able to use the red veil and other sisters who have left the Order."

Mimi thought about the implications. She said, "If I left the Order, would I be considered rogue?"

Noatla paused for a moment. It was Serah who spoke up. "Yes, and you better believe we'd watch your every move."

Noatla gave Serah a stern look. Then turned her eyes to Mimi. "Forgive Serah's bluntness, but yes, any sisters who depart from our company must be monitored."

Mimi clenched her fists. "And you just conveniently didn't tell me this when I signed up?"

"Can you blame us for being cautious after Miranda?"

Mimi thought about it and relaxed her fists just a little. "I guess not, but I would have liked to have known that in advance."

"Again, these are things that we do not share until you have a full understanding of your abilities and you know your sisters well. We are first and foremost watchers. We only intervene when the lives of those in the city are threatened. Can you tell us that if one of our sisters went rogue and began to hurt people, that you wouldn't want us to stop them?"

Mimi shook her head. "Fair. So, these sisters who specialize in the red veil, are there any here now?"

Shandie said, "Me. I am the only one right now."

Mimi regarded her carefully. She had paid little attention to the thin brown-haired and brown-eyed woman before. "Do you use it a lot?"

Shandie said, "No, almost never. I don't like it, it's like a drug, and after I always feel hung over. I would only use it in a dire emergency."

Noatla said, "Shandie has been with us for almost five centuries now, she is well-trained and well-liked among her sisters. She does not have an angry or hateful bone in her body, but if she went rogue, we would still need to watch her, to be sure she didn't do something horrible with her special talent."

Shandie said, "I do not take any of this lightly, Mimi. I have no desire to harm someone with my abilities, but I fully expect my sisters to stop me should I do something harmful."

Noatla said, "Mimi, it's time we focused on the problem at hand. Even though the circumstances are strange, that does not change the fact that we must find some kind of a solution to the problem, does it."

Vala, who had thus far remained silent, said, "But is there a solution?"

Mimi said, "There has to be. I'm not letting her go out into the Barrens to die. Not even if she is in one of those suits. I won't sit around and do nothing."

Serah said, "Muscle augmentation takes a solid forty-eight hours to take root. She will be boxed during that time, since the regenerative alcoves heal the damage that augmentation causes at the same time. However, they usually give Runners an extra two days in the alcoves to heal up, just in case. But again, in cases of emergencies, they would pull them after forty-eight. But there's certainly nothing going on that would warrant it."

"So then, we can get her out once the forty-eight hours are up," Mimi said.

"Yes, but again, the problem is the behavior chip. It tracks everywhere she goes."

"Is there a way to disable it?" asked Noatla.

"No. Not unless you have the clearance of that of Major Daniels, the chief of security, or maybe that loony city architect Solidsworth. They are probably the only ones in the city who could do something like that."

"So why can't we go and influence them to do this?"

Noatla shook her head. "Mimi, you still have much to learn. Influence only goes so far. Force, is the red veil. If the red veil is used, it could destroy the minds of both parties. This is why the red veil is forbidden. This is why Shandie would only use her powers in an emergency."

"Doesn't this qualify as an emergency?"

Shandie said, "Yes of course, and I would do everything in my power to help you, but the red veil is dangerous in this case."

Mimi said, "But why?"

Fatima said, "Both are very strong minds. Strong minds do not influence easily. The red veil has its limits. Not everyone can be controlled. In some cases, the person may only be frozen in place for a little time while they muster their will to push back. If the person pushes back and the red veil is not released, both are likely to die; it is too much for both minds."

"Can we influence them, then?" Mimi asked.

Noatla said, "These two are as Fatima said, well-established minds. Even if all of us worked together to influence them, the result may still not be what we wanted it. For example, if we pushed them to disable the behavior chip in Shannon, they may decide that they are disabling the chip because it isn't effective and simply have a new one installed. Older and more intelligent people are extraordinarily difficult to influence, and Major John Daniels and Dr. Rigel Solidsworth are the two oldest in Manhatsten. They are so old in fact, that they helped to raise the city onto its legs."

Mimi frowned. She felt the waves of the stormy sea of emotions. She wanted to shout, wanted to yell, but both were useless. These women were trying to help her, even if they weren't finding a solution.

Suddenly Serah jumped up. "Shit, I think I have a solution."

"What is it?" said Noatla.

Serah told them.

# Chapter 13
# The Runnercore

"YOU KNOW WHAT THIS building was before?" said Leahara.

Mimi shrugged. "No clue. Does it matter?" Her words were sharp.

Leahara winced a little and Shandie stiffened.

Mimi said, "Sorry. I'm just nervous."

The three sisters stood just outside an ancient building long after designated dark. It looked like some kind of museum to Mimi. Pillars were etched into the crumbling concrete, and an ancient clock with an inlaid golden sun marked the apex.

"It used to be called Grand Central Terminal," said Leahara.

"And now it's the entrance to the Runner Docks," said Mimi.

Shandie said, "Who told you that, Leahara?"

"Fatima. She studied ancient architecture in the scholar school."

Mimi felt a twinge of agitation. There were people in the city barely able to survive on their income, yet some people, just because of an accident of birth, could lounge around the highest parts of the skyscrapers and read books about buildings?

Leahara said, "I know, Mimi. I don't disagree with you. It doesn't seem justified, does it? I just thought it was interesting that this used to be a terminal for traveling around the city. Also, you need to learn to hide your thoughts a little better."

Mimi shrugged. "Do you think it's clear yet?"

"We wait for Serah. Clearing out the docks is difficult. There are quite a few people down there. We're lucky that the city hasn't needed to deploy any Runners for a few weeks. Only inspectors will be down there, and they are easier to persuade to leave. If our sisters do their job and persuade them all to leave, we shouldn't see anyone inside while we find our way to the Runner Storage Facility."

Mimi squirmed. There was so much that could go wrong with the plan. Serah had seemed confident she could pull it off. Mimi wasn't sure what it meant for her and Shannon even if they succeeded, but it would be far better than worrying about Shannon dying on some asinine mission out in the barrens or in city combat. More than anything, she wanted to hold Shannon and tell her how sorry she was. She hoped Shannon could forgive her. Besides, everything that had happened was Mimi's fault.

Shandie said, "Does that clock still work?"

Leahara reached back into a rear pocket and pulled out a small data tablet, glancing at the time. "No, look, the hands haven't moved at all, and we've been here twenty minutes."

Mimi said, "Serah's late."

Shandie said, "It's not easy to break into central security, you know. Even with Noatla and Fatima guiding her, she's a Runner. She can't be seen walking around in central security."

Mimi hadn't thought of that element. Serah was risking everything to help Shannon. Why would she do that? Shannon wasn't even part of the sisterhood.

"Leahara, why didn't you go with her? Couldn't you help her be less visible?"

"Fatima is proficient in stealth and Noatla didn't want anyone from the lowers up there while they were working. She said it would be enough trouble if Serah was recognized, that more bodies meant more chances to be noticed."

Mimi said, "I thought Fatima specialized in confusion, not stealth?"

"She does, but she's practiced at stealth too. Fatima is the oldest of us. She's picked up quite a few skill sets over the centuries."

Shandie said, "Look, here she comes." Serah rounded the corner and walked up to them.

"You ready?"

All three women nodded, and they walked through the double doors that led to a ground level of the station. The first area was still open to the public. During the day a few shopkeepers did business there. Most of the time, the area was the main checkpoint to enter the Runner Docks and nothing more.

No one met them in the space. The silence was interrupted only by the sounds of their feet on the ancient marble. They walked past one security checkpoint, but it was unmanned. The other sisters had done their job well.

They walked down through another pair of large doors; this area looked much newer. A long staircase descended toward the underground. Mimi had snuck in a few times before, but she had never found any kind of back entrance to the Runner Docks. The staircase was the only way in or out, and she thought that was purposeful.

The stairs opened to a long tunnel. Both directions led to the Runner Docks. They chose the left one and continued to walk in silence.

As they walked, Mimi almost tripped. The ground still had a few pieces of train track left on it. Most of the other pieces of the ancient subway were torn up and recycled to repair different parts of the city.

After a few minutes of walking, the tunnels opened into a large space. It was a concrete jungle. Above, mechanical arms lay dormant just above small raised platforms, and in the rim of the space were several small one-story concrete structures.

Serah said, "Home sweet home."

Mimi said, "What are those structures?" she pointed to the rim of the space. She had always wondered what all this stuff was. Now she had a tour guide.

"Those? That's where the inspectors hang out when they aren't deploying Runners."

"Deploying?"

"Yeah, so when one of us is activated, they unbox us from storage and we travel down one of the tunnels." Serah pointed to the various tube-like entrances that punctuated the wall toward the center of the city. "And then we come out and they inspect our body and mind and make sure we are ready to suit up."

"The arms and the platforms? That's where you suit up?"

"Yeah, you can put on an EnViro suit manually, but it's a pain in the ass. It's much easier to step up onto one of those platforms and let the arms dress you."

Shandie said, "So where's storage?"

"Technically, just up one of those tubes. But they're exit only. Less to guard that way. The Runners are vulnerable in the alcoves. There's only one entrance, and it's up this way." She pointed to the far end of the open space, several hundred meters away.

They walked without difficulty. A concrete desert, void of all life.

Serah said, "I'm always impressed with our sisters' abilities. I've never seen the place empty like this."

Mimi felt uneasy. She had expected some kind of resistance, and so had Noatla. It seemed strange that it was completely empty.

Mimi said, "I don't know, Serah. Something doesn't feel right. Maybe we should move a little quicker."

"Alright, but don't worry. This is my turf. Even if we do run into some resistance, I belong down here."

Shandie said, "Yes, but you're not supposed to be out of storage."

"True, but I don't think anyone will be that much trouble, not with four of us here."

They were halfway across when they saw the doors at the far end open up. Two figures came out. Both were in EnViro suits. Their metal forms moved at a slow and steady pace. They were coming toward them.

Serah frowned. "Recycled. Just keep your heads up and walk past them. They probably have orders from the AI."

"What exactly do they do down here?" asked Leahara.

"Routine shit, mostly. They carry out all the maintenance tasks that the AI needs done. I've heard of them fighting when they need to, but I hear they don't make great soldiers, they are slow to react. But if all you need to do is restrain a few Runners or have them act as a barrier to block someone from getting in or out, they're perfect."

Mimi watched as they moved closer. She felt a little more nervous with every step. Her heart raced. Her mind flashed back to the afternoon when she had hurt Shannon, of the image of Daniel reaching for her. She hoped to the gods that neither of those Runners were him.

Shandie asked, "How many of those things are there?"

Serah said, "No idea. It could be a few dozen or a few hundred. I'm not sure anyone knows."

Leahara said, "Who manages them all?"

Serah said, "The AI. Who else?"

Mimi said, "You trust the AI?" She had thought it benign most of her life, but seeing those things up close, knowing that it controlled them, she wasn't so sure. Maybe the AI was more intelligent than anyone knew, maybe it was biding its time.

Serah raised her hands, palms up. "Why wouldn't I? It's not like it's even fully aware. It's just a sophisticated computer program. And mine." She pointed to the back of her neck where a small bit of metal gleamed, "It's always with me, and it's served me well."

Mimi said, "You can talk to it now? Could you find out why those things are coming towards us?" Mimi eyed them. They were close enough now that their pale faces were taking shape. Already Mimi could see a hint of the blue lines that ran like race tracks around their skin.

"No, there has to be some sort of interface, like an EnViro suit or a computer terminal. The behavior chip just stores its memory and data. But I've been out in the Barrens a few dozen times now, and the AI kept me safe and alerted me of danger. So yeah, I'd say I trust it."

Silence fell over them as the creatures approached. Even a mind-to-mind communication seemed too loud, too obvious. Mimi closed her mind. A sealed vault. She was getting better, and after almost a week of regular practice, she found herself able to block most of her sisters so they couldn't always see her. They had told her it was a muscle.

The creatures were only a several meters away, and Mimi saw that neither of their faces were Daniel. She breathed a sigh of relief. She noticed a sharp pain in her palms and realized that she had been concentrating so hard that she had been digging her nails into her palms. She looked down and saw a hint of blood where reddened crescents marked her skin.

Mimi took a deep breath. She did her best not to look directly at the Recycled. Walking behind her other sisters now, she noticed that they too were keeping their head forward. All necks were rigid. Ships passing in the night.

As the creatures passed just in front of them, they stopped. Mimi felt a surge of panic. Did they notice them? She waited for them to turn and face her and her sisters, to reach out their hands, to clutch for her throat as Daniel had done in the dream. Neither did.

The four women adjusted their path, but the creatures stood frozen, staring towards the edge of the city.

Serah transmitted to Mimi's mind. "Keep walking. They're probably getting new orders. Sometimes they stop like that. It's creepy as hell but not unusual."

Mimi took another breath and kept walking. Her mind and body ached to turn toward those Recycled, to see if they were still behind them, but she refused.

A few minutes later they came to another set of large doors. They stopped and stood outside them. Mimi felt safe to glance back and did so. Both of the Recycled Runners had vanished.

Serah said, "Man I hate those things. Gods, I hope I never become one. I made Noatla promise that if I ever became one of those things that she would eliminate me. I don't know if there's anything human left in there, but sometimes I wonder if the person is inside and trapped."

Mimi didn't want to think about it. She said, "Is this the entrance to the storage facility?"

Serah said, "Yeah. We're near to where they would keep Shannon. The trick is finding her."

Leahara said, "What do you mean?"

Serah said, "You'll see."

IT WAS A WAREHOUSE of human bodies. For hundreds of meters, shelving stacked five levels tall were filled with sealed metal alcoves. Inside, human bodies floated in green goop. Clear window panels in metal frames gave glimpses of faces, feet, and arms on the first level, but higher up they could only guess at the occupants.

"Dear lord," said Leahara. "How many of them are there?"

Serah said, "No idea. A few thousand?"

Mimi said, "How... how in the hell do we find her?"

"The AI," said Serah. "AI, locate Runner 5444."

The voice of the AI said, "Runner 5444 is boxed in section 386 on level 2."

"Great. AI, unbox Runner 5444."

"Unable to comply, Runner 5444 cannot be removed from storage at this time. The post-op healing period is not yet complete."

"Well how long until the healing period is complete?"

"The healing period will be complete in eleven minutes and thirty-two seconds."

"AI, when the healing period is complete, unbox Runner 5444."

"Unable to comply. Authorization code required."

Serah rolled her eyes and said, "God you're a pain in the ass today. AI, use authorization code delta, five, six, one, nine, bravo, three, omega."

There was a pause for a moment.

"Authorization code accepted. Unboxing will commence in eleven minutes and three seconds."

"Come on, ladies," said Serah. "We got to get moving to section 387. It's a little bit of a walk."

THE THING THAT MIMI would remember most about that day, besides the horrific events that followed, was the sight of the claw picking up the alcove off the shelf and standing it upright on the grated metal floor. There was something about the machinery that caught in her memory. Later, she would tell Noatla that she couldn't believe how many machines and how much technology was down there when some buildings in the city were crumbling from disrepair.

Mimi watched as a few machines came to life and with soap and water, rinsing Shannon. A clear panel slid open letting Shannon out. When Shannon tried to step forward, she fell, but Mimi, eager to hold her in her arms, dashed forward and caught her.

Shannon looked up, her voice weak and frail. "Mimi. I'd knew you come for me." Shannon looked pale.

Serah said, "Be gentle with her, she's probably still recovering. Like I told you the other day, they usually give them four days to recover just to be on the safe side. Some people take a little longer to heal."

Shannon looked up at the surrounding faces. "Who are these women?"

Shannon, "These women... well... they are like me."

"Like you how? You mean... they can do the things you can with their minds?"

"Yes, and some of them can do much more."

"I thought you said you were alone."

"That's because I thought I was. I had no idea they existed until a week ago, until the day that... that..."

Mimi burst into tears. "Oh gods, Shannon, I'm so sorry. I never meant for any of this to happen to you. This is all my fault."

"Your fault? What are you talking about? How could this all be your fault?"

"I hurt you... I... scared you."

Shannon stared right into Mimi's eyes and then kissed her. "Love, that doesn't make what happened to me your fault. And I forgive you for scaring me. I know you would never hurt me on purpose." Shannon cried.

"Alright you two," said Serah, who looked uncomfortable, "we have to move."

Mimi blinked, wiped her eyes and helped Shannon stand. "Shannon, this is Leahara, Serah, and Shandie. They are... well... they are my sisters now."

Saying it out loud was strange to Mimi, but how could it be otherwise now? These women had all risked so much to help the woman she loved. Who else would do that but family? She thought on her mother, and how her mother had sacrificed everything for her, the way these women had.

Shannon looked at the women. "It's very nice to meet you all."

"Talk later," said Serah. "Right now, we only have thirty minutes to get the hell out of here before the inspectors come back; that evacuation drill won't last forever. So long as we are quick, that should be plenty of time, but I don't want to take chances."

"Where are we going?" asked Shannon.

"We are taking you to a new home," said Mimi.

THEY WERE HOME FREE. The exit to the storage facility opened into the main docks. As Mimi looked around, she saw it was still empty. No inspectors, no SOs or anyone else running around. The space was an open plain. There were no places for predators to hide.

Except there was.

As the five women walked out into the open, two Recycled Runners appeared. They were walking perpendicular, across the open space.

Shannon said, "I hate those things."

Mimi nodded but said nothing.

Serah said, "Like before ladies, they're creepy but harmless."

Shannon said, "Before?"

Mimi said, "We encountered two on the way in. They were creepy but didn't bother us."

Shannon replied, "They're really creepy. Wait, why are they stopping?" Her voice shook.

The creatures froze.

"Probably new order again," said Serah. "I told the others on the way, they do this all the time. It's nothing to worry about, Shannon."

"Then why are they walking towards us now?" said Shannon.

Mimi noticed that they had indeed resumed.

"Coincidence," said Serah. "I've walked by them a hundred times, and I've never had any issues."

But something about that didn't seem right to Mimi. It seemed like the creatures were walking towards them. Somehow it was different from last time. Mimi felt sweat gather on her forehead, felt her heart beating a little harder. She hoped that Serah was right, just like before, but her guts were screaming at her, saying that there was something very wrong.

The creatures approached. They were moving quick, much more quickly than they had the first time around.

Shannon said, "Can we walk around them? Please?"

Leahara said, "I agree with Shannon. Let's walk more to the left, even if it means it takes a little longer."

Serah rolled her eyes, "Alright, but we have to move quick. The inspectors won't be much longer, and we really should be out of here before then. The less we have to use our abilities down here, the better."

They rushed to the left to circle around the Recycled.

Then there were two more of the creatures coming toward them. Their appearance seemed more deliberate. When the women's path changed, so did the four creatures.

Mimi stopped and turned.

Behind them, six more Runners were walking their direction.

"Serah, look."

Serah did. She eyed her sisters. "It's a coincidence. It has to be."

For Mimi, the world tinged red.

"Serah, I can't move. It's..." the words could barely make it out of her. "The... red... veil..."

Shandie shouted something. It was fog at first but then clarified. The redness disappeared.

Then Serah ran. But she ran back toward the direction they had come, back towards storage. She was shouting something, but Mimi could only make out the words "AI" and "Platform."

Shandie grabbed Shannon's hand and then Mimi's. "Come on. We have to get out of here. Leahara, you know what you need to do."

Leahara closed her eyes for a moment and then followed behind. She said, "I've made us less visible, but I don't know if it will work on these creatures."

Mimi said, "Where in the world is Serah going?"

Leahara said, "I don't know. But she said we have to keep moving."

There were several dozen now, coming from every corner of the room. Every time Mimi looked, more were coming from the tubes that led to the storage facility. They streamed in from every door, moving swiftly with clear deliberation. Whenever Mimi and her sisters changed direction, so did the creatures. They still had at least two hundred meters to cross the space, and Mimi was certain that there was no way they could make it without being surrounded.

The creatures closed in. There were at least a hundred now. The closest were only a few dozen meters away, but still more streamed in.

Shannon sobbed. "They're coming for me, Mimi. They're coming for me. Let me go back or they'll hurt us." Shannon stopped for a moment and crouched on the ground, clutching her head. "Why is everything red? What's happening? Mimi, is this you?"

Mimi felt a pang of guilt, knowing that if she was experiencing the red veil, that it must be like what Mimi had done to her.

"Oh god, make it stop, Mimi. Make it stop."

Mimi tried to pull her to her feet, but she wouldn't budge.

Shandie said, "Hush Shannon, what you're hearing isn't real. It's a lie. Ignore it. The headache will pass if you keep moving. Do not stop." Her words were firm and powerful, and Shannon stood. She wobbled as she did, but Mimi grabbed her arm and steadied her.

Mimi said, "Come on, once we get out of here, we'll be safe. Let's hurry." Mimi wasn't sure that was true, but she knew Shannon need to hear it.

It was too late. The first two Recycled Runners stood before them. Two others were only a few meters away. The creatures formed a circle of hybrid reanimated flesh-and-metal bodies. In moments, the four women were flanked. Penned animals.

Mimi pushed Shannon behind her. The other two sisters put their bodies between Shannon and the Recycled. For a moment, nothing happened. Then, the sound of a solitary set of metal footsteps on concrete punctuated the silence outside the circle. Two of the Recycled parted. A gate. A hell-gate. Through the opening, a singular Recycled Runner stepped forward into the circle.

Mimi saw his face. Her whole body trembled. Her legs almost gave out, and she gripped Shannon's arms tight.

Just above a whisper, Mimi said, "Oh gods. It's..."

No more words would come. Mimi's mouth opened and shut, but she was frozen in place. The red veil tinged everything. She could feel a trickle of drool escape the corner of her mouth. Her muscles locked. A statue, a monument.

It was Daniel. His skin was almost translucent, marked with blue lines where the veins had been. He was a shadow, a living ghost, a reminder of all the pain Mimi had felt, of all the pain Mimi had caused. Daniel had survived his transformation into a runner. He had gone out on his first mission, and a storm had killed him. They recovered the body and had converted him to this thing. It was why she feared Shannon leaving the city in one of those suits.

Shannon tugged at her arm, but Mimi remained immobile. Her mind had gone blank as the empty white eyes stared into hers. There was no pupil, no sign that there was anything behind the blank white surface in the Recycled Runner's eyes, and yet she felt she could not look away. Flashes of red light. Fireworks in her vision.

It stepped a little closer, raising its arm. Its hand opened. The shape of a claw. A perfect fit for Mimi's neck. Daniel would know its tenderness. She saw what would happen. She saw it would crush her windpipe and then lift her on its shoulders and take it to the place where it was born.

In her mind, Mimi saw as a drill descended from above, screaming its angry motion as it pierced her forehead. The smell of burning bone licked her nostrils as it dug deeper.

Shannon was shaking her. She was screaming. It was distant though, like thunder trumpeting the horizon a thousand miles away. The image of the drill vanished as Shannon slapped her and tried to yank her from where she stood. No movement. She felt the heat of Shannon's hand a second time, but could not move.

The creature reached her. It slide its fingertips around the edge of Mimi's throat. And, as if expecting a soft silken glove, Mimi tilted her chin up, ready to accept the metal hand and the invitation to become a part of their legion.

Then, Leahara was there. She threw her body against the creature, but it did nothing. The metal suit weighed hundreds of kilos and Leahara only staggered it. It stood watching, unmoving, waiting, considering.

Its metal gauntlet expanded, the fingers widened, and it reached out and gripped Leahara by the top of the head. Metal fingers squeezed. Mimi could only observe. It was like watching a vid screen as she heard her sister scream in agony.

Shandie ran up and tried to knock the arm loose, but the creature that had been Daniel swatted her away with little effort. Shandie hit the ground and smacked the back of her head on the concrete. Her eyes closed.

Its fingers tightened, and Mimi could hear Leahara's skull groaning under the pressure. It was a sound she would remember for the rest of her days. The Recycled lifted her off the ground with only its single arm. The other dangled at its side. Leahara's legs kicked as it raised her up. Then with a quick jerk of its wrist, it wrenched Leahara's head to the side. Mimi heard a terrifying snap, and Leahara's body went limp. The creature dropped it, letting the body fall to the floor.

Shannon shrieked.

Mimi thought of her training. The red veil was still over her, but it seemed a little weaker now. She tried with all of her might to reach into the creatures' minds, to implant suggestions to them, but there was no use. Someone or something was controlling them.

There was the clash of metal. The noise ruptured the veil and Mimi was free to move again. She looked over, and someone in one of the large metal suits was crashing its way through the Recycled. Armed with a long blade, it severed the head of the creature that was Daniel, unprotected as it was, it dropped to the ground. A fountain of blue liquid pumped from the creature's neck.

Serah shouted into Mimi's mind, and it almost knocked her off her feet. "Run, dammit!"

The woman moved with a grace and a speed that Mimi wouldn't have thought possible in one of the large metal suits. The suit crouched down and then, with a hard push from the legs, jumped up into the air and flipped backward, sweeping a blade across two more of the Recycleds' necks.

They turned her attention to Serah. Mimi knew there were too many. She guessed that there had to be more than a hundred now. All moved toward Serah, who, despite their numbers, appeared to be taking them down, one after another. Then, several of the creatures broke into a run and moved with incredible speed. They knocked Serah off her feet for a moment. She rolled in the suit and jumped back up.

"I said run, you asshole!" Serah shouted again. "I got this."

Mimi knew that was a lie, but she grabbed Shannon by the hand and ran over to Shandie. Her mouth was open, her eyes closed, and Mimi checked for a pulse. There was none. She noticed a large puddle of blood under her head. The creature had killed her with almost no effort.

It was too much. Rage came then. Mimi saw red. But this red did not come from the outside of her; it came from the inside. It poured out of her as she focused her mind on one of the Recycled. One creature that had been moving steadily toward Serah fell to its knees and screamed in agony for a moment and then dropped with a large crunch, face first into the concrete. Mimi focused on two more, and they too fell to the ground until they lay motionless.

Several dozen of the creatures shifted their focus from Serah to Mimi. For a moment, the red in her burned like a newly formed star, but as more creatures turned their attention to her, anger evaporated, and fear replaced it. There were too many, and now they were interested again.

She looked at Shannon, whose eyes were like glass, whose mouth gaped open at her. She could tell what Shannon was thinking. Shannon remembered how Mimi had entered her mind and there was terror in Shannon's face.

Mimi felt the guilt but shook her head. "Later. Let's go." Regardless of what Shannon thought of her now, she couldn't let anything happen to her.

They ran. Behind them, the sounds of combat continued as Serah did her best to stop the reanimated army.

But it wasn't enough. There were too many and only one Runner. Mimi wished that she knew how to pilot one of those suits.

The exit was close then, only a few dozen meters away. Running as fast as they could, they reached the base of the steps and stopped. More of the creatures poured in from the exit, a wall of recycled flesh and metal. Shannon and

Mimi retreated a few steps and turned to look back, remembering that Serah had said this was the only exit. She looked for something, anything to help defend herself or hide behind. There was nothing.

As she turned back toward the exit, the noises of combat behind evaporated. She glanced back and saw that the creatures had Serah pinned and were trying to tear her armor off.

They were trapped. This time, all the creatures descended at once. She knew they would leave nothing to chance this time. Mimi grabbed Shannon and pulled her close.

"I love you Shannon. I'm so sorry for everything."

"I love you too Mimi, and I'm sorry too."

Both wept as the circle closed. The air seemed to compress around them. It became hard to breathe.

One creature grabbed Mimi by the arm and pulled her away from Shannon. She resisted, but its hand was strong. Mimi felt something snap under the stress of its power and she cried out in pain, her arm broken. She did not take her eyes off of the woman she loved, and as the creature dragged her away, she held Shannon's hand with all of her strength. But it wasn't enough. She felt their hands part.

"Run Shannon. Please. Run. Get out of here."

But before Shannon could move, another creature grabbed her and dragged Shannon in the same direction as Mimi.

Mimi looked up at the creature's face, the one that had her. It was smiling. Hungry rows of sharpened teeth bared for all to see.

In that same moment, its smile vanished. It shook its head back and forth, slowly at first and then much more rapidly.

The creature dropped her broken arm. It shrieked and fell to its knees. Mimi looked up at Shannon, she too had been released, and the creature that had held her was in the same kneeling position, shrieking in the same high-pitched wail. A chorus from hell.

Then they were there. Around her. All of them. Her sisters picked her up with great care and Noatla and Fatima walked toward the hoard of reanimated Runners.

There was fury in both women's eyes. Fury that Mimi had never thought possible with those two. Their faces were both darkened with rage. Eyes of lighting. As they walked towards Serah's downed metal suit, the creatures that didn't flee fell to their knees. Four other sisters joined the march and Mimi, despite her broken arm, ran to join them. With her sisters, she pushed on the mind of the creatures and one by one they either fell in agony or scattered to the corners of the massive underground area, fleeing in many directions.

The creatures were gone. Dozens of their bodies lay on the floor, most face down with a trickle of blue liquid leaking from their ears. The blue fluids gathered in puddles around the room.

They reached Serah. Sister Vala helped her out of the EnViro suit. She was alive, but she had one of her arms and both of her legs broken. Vala and Patricia picked her up and carried her as Noatla inspected the body of Leahara, and Fatima inspected the body of Shandie.

The sisters of the Order of the Eye gathered their dead and their wounded and departed to the safety of the lower library.

# Chapter 14
# Cold Storage

FOUR DAYS PASSED. MIMI lay awake in her hovel, alone, her arm healed from an alcove. She reviewed the events of the last month. She couldn't believe so much had happened in such a short period, not when the centuries had stretched out so long into her past.

That morning, the order held a memorial service for Sister Shandie and Sister Leahara in the library. At the end, they burned the bodies so there was never any chance of them being recycled. Lots of shed tears and shared stories. For Mimi, a lot of guilt.

Over and over again, her sisters told her that Leahara and Shandie's deaths were not their fault, that if they had known what would happen, they would have all went in together. That none of them could know the future.

Still, she had struggled at the memorial service. But she spoke of her short but meaningful friendship with Leahara and how Leahara had reached out to her and made Mimi feel welcome. Now, Mimi felt like a part of the sisterhood. That wasn't the problem.

There was a flash of another mind. For a moment it was jumbled and then she recognized it. She threw on some clothes and stepped out of her hovel.

"Evening, Mimi. How are you feeling?" said Noatla, her voice even.

Mimi shrugged. "I don't know. How am I supposed to feel?"

Noatla moved forward and embraced her. It was the first time the Matron had ever done so.

Noatla said, "It's time to go see her. We will go together, you and me. I wish to speak with you at length."

Mimi nodded. They walked.

When they reached the pipe they had to crawl through to get out, Noatla said, "How in the hell do you climb through this all the time?"

Mimi smiled and shrugged. "I guess I've been crawling through this pipe for so long I don't even think about it. Also, you have at least a foot on me in height. It was never easy for Shannon, either. At least she won't have to worry about it now." Mimi's smile evaporated.

"She'll be okay now. It may take getting used to for both of you, but she will be alright."

Mimi nodded. But it didn't make her feel any better. She wished it could be how it was before, those few short weeks when she and Shannon had spent every waking moment together. She longed for it.

They crawled out the other side and paused a moment at the staircase that led up to the street level of the city.

Mimi said, "Noatla, will you wait for a few minutes? There is something I need to get."

Noatla nodded. Mimi flew up the steps and sprinted out onto the streets.

MIMI RETURNED A FEW minutes later with a small package under her arm.

Noatla glanced at it. "You know you could get in a lot of trouble for that." But the smile never left Noatla's face.

Mimi shrugged and shared her own smile.

Noatla led Mimi down another corridor. It was the remains of an ancient subway line. It was dimly lit, and many of the lights were long burnt out, others flickered. Mimi had walked down it before, had explored it looking for salvage, but when she had found nothing, she had not bothered going down it again. After several long kilometers, it came to a thick metal door that Mimi had never got through.

They walked for a while without words. The surrounding bedrock cultivated silence.

Noatla broke the silence. "We need you now. I hope you felt it when you stood with your sisters and drove those creatures back. We need you now more than ever. It will take time to find new sisters."

"Noatla... I..." Mimi paused and took a breath. She kicked an old rock along the track, the sound echoed. "Don't you see, Matron? I'm cursed. Everyone I have ever gotten close to is dead or have had their lives destroyed. I'm like a shadow, like a thing that blocks out the light in the world and now..." She was crying. "Now, Leahara and Shandie are dead, Serah only just barely survived, and Shannon's life will never be the same." Her voice quavered.

Mimi stopped walking as she felt a hand touch her shoulder. Then Noatla embraced her again and held her for several minutes while the tears streamed down the side of her cheeks. She could taste the salt and let her chest heave as she wept.

When Mimi calmed, Noatla broke the embrace but grabbed Mimi's hands and held them. Mimi looked up into Noatla's big blue eyes, and the woman was smiling at her.

"Mimi, all shadows are cast by light. There is a moment, a chance, when you face your greatest darkness, that you can turn, just a little bit, and trace the source of the shadow unto its origin. It is in those moments you have the chance to understand something about yourself and about the world that you may have never seen before. The darkness of your past is an opportunity. You are not the things that have happened to you. You are not your talents or your weakness, you are what you choose to be. There is no shadow you can cast that love, friendship, and kindness cannot overcome. Stay with us Mimi, let us help you see that you are not a shadow, but a powerful source of light."

Mimi didn't know what to say. So, instead, she resumed walking. She thought again about all that had happened. About all the pain she had seemed to cause, but it seemed different somehow. She looked up at Noatla, eyes suspicious.

"Are you soothing me?"

"Only a little, Mimi. I don't want you to be overwhelmed. If you like, I'll stop. But I promise I am only trying to let your emotions rest a little. They've had quite an ordeal recently."

Mimi thought about it, "No... it's alright. It's helping. I feel like my mind is clear for the first time in days."

"Good, that was my intention."

Mimi nodded. A thought occurred to her.

"Did we find the Recycled? What happened to all those bodies?"

Noatla's demeanor shifted a little. She tried to hide it, but Mimi saw the ghost of that same fury she had seen when Noatla had attacked the Recycled. "No Mimi, many of them have disappeared. Vala, Patricia, and Rebecca have been searching all of the underground, but several dozen are unaccounted for. The others we found have yielded no clues to what happened. As for the bodies, we managed to convince the inspectors that it was a serious malfunction in their suits and a clean-up and engineering team has been combing the Runner Docks for the last few days."

"Do you think it was... that woman? That Miranda?"

Noatla sighed. For a moment Mimi didn't think she would answer. Noatla almost never showed any signs of impatience, at least not from what Mimi could tell, but here was one. Noatla recovered herself.

"Forgive my impatience, Mimi. It's just that I have had this same conversation with several other of your sisters already. Some insist it is the only explanation for what happened while others insist that Miranda is long dead."

"And what do you think, Matron?"

"I think it is a bad idea to take anything off the table right now. I think it takes someone of extraordinary power to control that many Recycled in such an efficient way. I think that only someone who was furious with us would attack us like that and I think besides Miranda, I am not sure if I know anyone who meets all that criteria."

"So you think it was her."

"I don't know, Mimi. When Mex fell, there was another group of people that Miranda worked with that we thought were gone. But we have been hearing rumors from other cities that they're still operating."

"Who are they?"

"They were known, or perhaps, are known, as the Children of Gaia. They are...well, they seek to destroy of all the cities. The Order of the Eye was founded to combat them, to stop them from destroying what's left of humanity when migration began. They worked with Miranda before the fall of Mex and we, perhaps in our optimism, thought both threats had ended and that we could be content with watching and making sure the city was safe. Perhaps this was foolish. It need not be Miranda if the Children of Gaia have returned. For Miranda was not the only rogue sister amongst their ranks."

"So you are saying they're in the city? These Children of Gaia?"

"I'm saying that perhaps simply watching may be at an end. We must be more vigilant, and we must not hesitate at anything suspicious or strange. Most of all, we must replenish our ranks, and we must not lose the ones who are already among us. We really do need you right now, especially since you have such an unusual talent. I have some... missions for you."

"Missions?"

"Yes, since you can skim technical information, there are things in the city we could learn and use to our advantage later."

Mimi nodded. She said nothing in reply, but she knew how Noatla was watching her.

"Matron, what about the AI? Could it be causing some of this?"

Noatla considered this for a moment, then said, "If somehow the AI were fully aware, it would certainly have the resources to control so many of those creatures efficiently. And we don't know the process of how they create the Recycled in the first place." Noatla paused for a moment and then smiled. "You see Mimi, this is exactly why we need you. This kind of investigation is suited for your particular skill set."

Mimi said nothing, but she hungered for answers.

Then they were at the door.

Noatla said, "AI, would you unlock the door please?"

"Senator Noatla Lightfoot, I am sorry, but an access code is required for entry."

"My access code is 8426FPA,"

"Thank you, Senator."

The door slid open.

IT WAS A MEDIUM-SIZED space, but the ceiling was several meters high, giving the room a strange resonance. On the edges of the room were small platforms. Each platform had an EnViro Suit standing on it, waiting for an occupant. Many alcoves stood in the circle, surrounding a central console. Thick cords ran from each of the alcoves to an electric box. The alcoves were slanted at a 45-degree angle. Faces showed from inside.

At the console stood Serah. Her flaming red hair was braided halfway down her back. She was busy at work and didn't seem to notice Mimi and Noatla come in.

Noatla said, "All healed up?"

Serah turned. She seemed just as strong as ever. "Yeah, the alcoves mended the bones quickly. They were clean breaks, so it was an easy fix."

Mimi asked, "Is she...?"

"Sleeping still, but it's almost time to wake her. It turns out her muscles weren't fully healed from the procedure, and since we took her out a little too early, I want to make sure we don't repeat the same mistake."

"Alright. So what's the plan again? She stays down here?"

"Yeah, we can keep her boxed here. But we can't let her go free. She can't leave the immediate area. Probably she could walk a few hundred meters in any direction, but more than that and the AI would track her in a heartbeat."

"If we keep her boxed down here," said Serah, "and we log her as a reserve, she can remain on ice for the time being. I'm sorry Mimi, there's not much more we can do. She can come out sometimes, but probably not more than a few days a month. The good news is, she will be safe here for now. Until things change in this city, there isn't much else I can offer. I know this isn't ideal, but..."

"But at least it's something," said Mimi. "Thank you, Serah. Is it possible for me to get full access to this place?"

Noatla said, "I can work on that. I had to skim my code from the head of city security, and it wasn't easy. Because I'm a Senator I have higher clearance, but I am sure we can figure something out. If nothing else, I will walk you down here whenever I can."

Serah said, "You know, we were lucky we got her in here so quickly. When Fatima and Noatla disabled the beacon to her chip, it was only a short-term measure, and we almost ran out of time. The AI updates its alerts every twenty-four hours. It's a fail-safe mechanism to ensure that alerts never go unnoticed in case they're turned off. The clock had just about reset when we arrived."

"Why this place? What is it?"

"It's a kind of emergency backup plan. Only a handful of people know about it. But if you notice, every single one of these alcoves is full, except one. Mine. This is how I can be a Runner and be a part of the sisterhood. I only sometimes go out on missions, mostly I can stay here."

Mimi asked, "So why are you able to leave but not Shannon?"

"Well, I have it rigged so that if I get assigned to a task, the activation alert comes here or, I get a notification straight to my chip if I'm not in my alcove. But you don't want Shannon to go out on any missions, so it means she has to be more hidden."

"Ah." Mimi fingered her package. Serah glanced at it but said nothing.

The console beeped. Serah turned and said, "Alright, she's cooked."

Serah pressed a button, and the bottom of Shannon's alcove tilted upright. It slid open, letting the fluids drain first down through a metal grate just below it. Then the alcove triggered a kind of shower mode, and it rinsed Shannon's body clean of all the green stem-cell-based gel. The door then slid fully open.

Shannon stepped out. She blinked and looked around for a second. Then her eyes surveyed the faces of those waiting.

"Mimi!"

Mimi moved forward. A nervous suitor, picking up her date for the time. She held the package out to her.

Shannon's face was all smiles. She took the package and unwrapped it. "Mimi... is this..."

Mimi nodded "Yes, just like you always wanted."

Shannon raised the roses up to her nose and inhaled. "But how did you get them? What if you got caught, I..."

Then they were in each other's arms, trading kisses and longing stares.

Shannon was crying. Mimi was crying. Tears mingled in the warmth of each other's embrace.

Shannon said, "It's better than being out in an EnViro suit. You know?"

Serah watched the two lovers embrace and replied, "I'll still train you in one, Shannon."

Shannon glanced at Serah, "But why?"

"Because I tricked the AI into thinking you were trained and you are considered a reserve Runner, one only brought out in a significant city emergency. The other ones here have the same status. They're put down here in case something happens to the entire Runnercore and the city needs backups. Only the AI knows about them. Possibly someone else does too, but central security at least is ignorant."

"You need to be ready, in case the worst case happens and we aren't able to keep you hidden. If you get pulled into active duty, I want you to be able to fight. If you're well-trained, then at least we have a backup plan."

Noatla asked, "How likely is something like this to happen, do you think, Serah?"

"You would know better than I, Noatla. How many times has the city been in a total state of emergency?"

Noatla considered. "Only a handful over the centuries."

"There you go, we need to make sure you are ready for one of those times. Besides, it might be nice to have someone else fight by my side in an emergency. Could have used you back at the Docks."

Mimi asked, "Can I train too?"

Serah said, "I can train you in hand-to-hand combat, at least. But the thing is, for you to get in one of these suits, you need to have your muscles augmented, and I'm not sure there is any way we can get a hold of what's needed without having you entered into the Runnercore program."

Shannon said, "No Mimi, I don't want you to go through what I have. You don't understand how painful it is. I can't bear to think of you going through that."

Mimi cast her eyes downward. "But you did it."

"Exactly, so I know just how awful it is, and I won't let you do it."

She lifted Mimi's chin and stole another kiss.

Shannon took another whiff of the flowers.

Mimi said, "Do you like them?"

Shannon smiled and then leaned forward and kissed Mimi's forehead. "Like them? I love them. I never imagined someone would bring me flowers. Not really."

"I'll bring you flowers every single time I come down."

Shannon frowned. "I don't know if that's a good idea, Mimi. I... I wouldn't want you to get in trouble."

"I'll be okay. Don't worry about me. I want to see that smile on your face."

Shannon hugged her tight.

THE VISIT LASTED MOST of the day before Serah had to put Shannon back into the alcove. Serah had told them that they could return tomorrow, and next time Mimi and Shannon could have some alone time.

Mimi and Noatla walked down the ancient subway tunnel back towards Mimi's hovel.

Noatla said, "So will you stay with us?"

"Yes. I think I will. If you need me, if Shannon needs me to help keep this city safe so there aren't any emergencies, then yes."

Noatla smiled, "That's wonderful to hear, Mimi. When will you be moving in with one of us? You are always welcome in my quarters. I can get you a guest pass, and you can live in the Uppers. You would never have to worry about your safety again."

Mimi shook her head. "Thank you, Noatla. That is more than generous. But I don't think I want to leave my home. Down here is my place. During my initiation, I told you, I was Mimi of the Nowhere. But the thing is, this is my Nowhere. It always has been. I don't think I can leave it behind just like that."

"And there is no way I can change your mind."

"You told me that the Order of the Eye is there to help the city, it is there to protect the city and watch over it, right?"

Noatla nodded.

"Noatla, who's been watching out for the homeless in this city? Who's been making sure that the SOs or the drug dealers don't abuse them? Which sister steps in and tries to help them whenever they become victims of the corruption of this city?"

Noatla cast her eyes downward. Mimi knew the answer.

"For too long, those who are from nowhere in this city have been ignored. I will stay among you, I will do your missions and aid you and my fellow sisters in any way I can, but I will also do my best to use my abilities to protect those who have no one and nothing."

Noatla looked at Mimi long and hard. "Mimi, I knew you would fit well into our order. I knew that your heart was in the right place. Do you see now the light behind the shadow?"

Mimi shrugged.

Noatla said, "You have my full support."

Mimi winked and then smiled. "As if I needed it."

They both laughed.

# Epilogue

SHE OPENED HER ALCOVE and climbed in. It had taken all of her effort to return alive. The Order of the Eye had grown strong in her absence. But, her strength would return in time. And there were always new vermin to be recycled.

Her forces were gathering again in the southwest. She was their goddess and they her children. A few decades and they would be ready. By then, she will have recovered her full strength. When she finished, not a single city would remain. When she finished, the great migration would end.

# Don't miss out!

Click the button below and you can sign up to receive emails whenever Michael Kilman publishes a new book. There's no charge and no obligation.

https://books2read.com/r/B-A-ZUBG-NOMS

BOOKS 2 READ

Connecting independent readers to independent writers.

# About the Author

Michael Kilman is an anthropologist who occasionally visits other worlds and reports back what he finds. When he isn't writing fiction he is lecturing at a few universities in the Denver metro area, or working on his YouTube series 'Anthropology in 10 or Less.' Michael can be found at his website, loridianslaboratory.com, and on Twitter at @LoridiansLab.

Read more at https://loridianslaboratory.com.

10752375R00084

Made in the USA
Lexington, KY
01 October 2018